SID SMITH

CHINA DREAMS

PICADOR

First published 2007 by Picador
an imprint of Pan Macmillan Ltd
Pan Macmillan, 20 New Wharf Road, London N1 9RR
Basingstoke and Oxford
Associated companies throughout the world
www.panmacmillan.com

ISBN 978-0-330-48125-0 HB
ISBN 978-0-330-45017-1 TPB

1 3 5 7 9 8 6 4 2

A CIP catalogue record for this book is available from
the British Library.

Typeset by SetSystems Ltd, Saffron Walden, Essex
Printed and bound in Great Britain by
Mackays of Chatham plc, Chatham, Kent

Visit www.panmacmillan.com to read more about all our books
and to buy them. You will also find features, author interviews and
news of any author events, and you can sign up for e-newsletters
so that you're always first to hear about our new releases.

CHINA DREAMS

1

He kept dreaming about China.

At first they were only daydreams: he pictured himself in a rice field, or he was leading his buffalo home under the stars, singing although he was tired, or he was fishing from a boat on a river, the fish very strange and Chinese. But then they were real sleeping dreams, and he'd snort and twitch and think that he'd never get home. And finally Tom saw that the dreams had a meaning, although to find the meaning always seemed to need another dream.

It started with May Tan, their room over her dad's takeaway, and his job on the little red delivery bike, wobbling down the Whitechapel Road with fried rice and crackers. Because of May he saw himself in China, happy with her in the jungle lowlands, or the wooded hills, or in the mountains near Tibet. But then she dumped him, and Tom thought the China dreams were over.

Instead he was back at the squat. He'd lived there the summer before, when he'd just left school and everyone was brown and the apple tree in fruit in the back garden. It was hot in his top-floor room so he'd sat under the tree, smoking dope and eating apples with students and hippies, signing for his dole with hands oily from fixing cars in the gutter. But now it was winter, and he had the clammy basement room, and the squat was full of ex-cons who didn't flush the toilet.

But the China thing went on. If he was out, there were always Orientals who might or might not be Chinese, and if he stayed indoors, sitting in the sleeping bag with his back against the concrete basement wall, he thought about May, her brother and dad, and the two cooks who couldn't describe China, or what it was like to be Chinese in London, and had edged him out of the takeaway on that last day, saying, 'You go,' and 'No trouble,' Tom dizzy with bad dope, and May wouldn't see him.

So he pictured her in China. She was on a buffalo. She was riding by a river, coming to their wedding. She wore a tall hat and a skirt of many layers. She was riding side-saddle on the way to the wedding, but afterwards she'd be astride. The ceremony was strange, but May's dad was helping. Tom and May walked into the river. They were married when they held hands under the water.

2

Tom's eyebrows were very black. They were always raised, even when he was alone. They made pointed arches over his eyes, and said that life was surprising and needed careful thought. In the street, people noticed these eyebrows and his wayward gaze, looking at cars or pigeons or women. His wiry black hair stood up in clumps.

All this was funny and endearing, as was his company. He spoke softly and quickly in his country accent, but preferred to listen, his mouth a little open, his eyebrows high, because people were mysteries he might puzzle out. He hated his tobacco teeth, so his smile was tight-lipped and shy, with the glance downwards.

Then May dumped him and he changed. His eyebrows were still high and surprised, but now they also showed hurt and sometimes anger. He watched people with suspicion, because they might betray him. And when he was alone he pined for May and their room under the eaves.

Tom liked the night, so he'd liked the takeaway. At first he'd worked the counter, but he bungled the orders and fumbled the change, so they sent him to the kitchen, where he broke plates, spilled sauce, and lost spoons in the noodles.

Then they put him on deliveries and forgave him everything because he'd go to the worst council blocks, not leaving the motorbike to be stolen or wrecked but riding up the stairwells over silver paper and used needles, and if a gang was waiting he wanted them to start something, staring them down until the ambush calls stopped.

On his days off he imagined being Chinese: in shops he'd point and nod, not speaking; he was careful on buses, like the Chinese cooks going home in their cheap clothes, London strange to him; and he'd sit in Chinatown cafes over green tea and bean-curd cakes, watching kids flirt and laugh, although their race is beyond age. When he was working he kept the bike helmet on, so that people might think he was Chinese.

After closing time he'd wheel the bike into the shed, where the watchdog shivered among turds and dried-up leftovers and pushed its nose in his hands to be stroked. He helped with the washing up, then ate leftovers at the steel-topped table with May's dad and the two cooks: Mr Tan dealing games of Patience with his creepy thick hairless arms, Chung big and absent-minded, little Wei sucking chicken bones, and Tom understanding nothing, watching their lips and eyes, hearing his name like a dog does, his arms on the cold table, his chin near his arms, smoking Marlboros from the big semi-legal packs in the cupboard under the sink and staring at the three Chinese, while newly washed pans dripped from a rack above the table. Big Chung was irritated to be watched, Wei amused, and Mr Tan thought that Tom was a fool.

Sometimes Johnny was home from college, May's nearly twin, nervous and snooty, propped against the cupboards. But most of all there was May, thin like Johnny, a girl by omission, arms folded over her trainee-nurse's blouse, joking with the cooks, her big black shoes at ten-to-two, giggling when Tom's eyebrows turned her way.

One night he was climbing on the bike when she said, 'Looks like fun.' He tapped the seat and she pulled up her nurse's skirt and jumped on, and this was his dream so he was drunk with lust before they'd left the yard, her skinny bum squeezed between his back and the plywood box for the food, and she was bouncing on the seat shouting, 'Faster, faster.'

For weeks they went all over London on the little red Honda, weaving up hills at walking speed, down alleys and pavements, through shopping precincts, warm in the late-summer nights, and then she'd use Johnny's line about getting from A to Beer, so he'd park outside pubs, proud of his China girl, and she was instantly drunk, red-faced and loving, laughing at her country boy, her hand light on his leg, her clever quick London voice. She'd doze on his shoulder all the way home, sleepy in the kitchen with the tired cooks, the plots and plans, eating leftovers under the strip lights, daring her dad to object, her dad saying, 'You poyfriend? Poyfriend?' then up the stairs for a snog in her room under the roof, decorated like the takeaway – red walls, tassels on the lampshade, Chinese travel posters, a velvet throw on the bed that maybe didn't squeak – until finally she let him stay.

On their last night together she was very drunk. He wheeled the bike into the shed and couldn't resist a quick oil check and brake-cable adjustment and a stroke of the dog, then up the stairs but her room was empty because she was snoring at the kitchen table between the two cooks that snobby Johnny called Eeny-Meeny and Miney-Mo. Or Fee-Fo and Fi-Fum. Or Who-How and Why-Where. Then he heard people on the stairs, but it was May stumbling and muttering. She fell into her room and undressed in a three-legged race with her jeans and fell on the bed, saying, 'Just wait till the Chinks take over.'

'That's why I'm reading this stuff.' Shelves of picture books about China, muddy colours on cheap paper, bought by her dad for a dozen birthdays but ignored.

She said, 'We'll call it the Yellowchapel Road. And we'll repaint the White House.'

'Yerrow?'

'And Whitehall.'

'I could be your slave and concubine.'

But she was sleeping, so he looked at pictures of a grinning ploughman, the Great Wall, cormorant fishermen with their lamps, and then imagined himself in China. May tended their little field, and he worked a claypit in a bend in the river. All day he drove a buffalo round and round to tread the clay. He hated the buffalo because it stepped in its old footholes.

The two cooks woke him. They tapped on May's door and took him to the all-night pool hall at King's Cross, where he picked up their splayed-finger cue action and gangster smoking style – the bared teeth, stiff fingers, shrewd frown, and wide enveloping swoop for the ashtray – then slept on the first Tube back to Brixton. He grabbed his dole, scored, had a day-long pub crawl, did deliveries all night, stoned stupid, and by ten was back at the takeaway.

The kitchen door was locked. He banged and shouted, then went round the front, and the two cooks were behind the counter with his sleeping bag. 'You go,' said big Chung, and little Wei said, 'No trouble,' edging him on to the street.

'Hang on. What's happened?'

'Don't come,' said Chung, pushing him with the doss bag. 'No phone, no come. Never, never. OK?'

So he sat in a pub, the bike key on its slinky wire on his wrist, still senseless with dope. The doss bag was full of his stuff. By closing time he was angry. He hid in the alley till the takeaway was dark, then broke a window and got into the shed, the dog whining and barking as he kick-started the bike for the long ride back to the squat.

Only the basement was free. There was a mattress on the concrete floor, and he bought a kettle and tea bags and dried milk. He stole a light bulb from a pub, a cup and spoon from a caff, and clear plastic sheeting off a building site, fixing it with thumbtacks round the cracked window. Someone had taken the door, but he claimed his big electric fire from a whining skinny ex-con upstairs, who said, 'You can't leave stuff and then take it back,' but left a week later after some sort of fight.

During the fight a wardrobe burst in the back yard, then a chair, and then a curtain rocked down and settled on the mess. Tom got the wet curtain to pin in his doorway, but instead he put it over the window because he was mostly asleep.

There was no catch on the house front door and for a while he propped it closed at night. But a ginger Scouse drunk always came in late and kicked it open, stumbling down the basement steps and spraying wildly in the toilet next to Tom's room. So the house door stayed open and Tom curled fully clothed in his sleeping bag against the draughts that flowed down the steps and gave his doorless room a campsite feel, the fire going day and night on the fiddled meter, while he lay in the gloom behind the curtain, imagining China.

He was a blacksmith. His forge was half underground, a blackened hole for a chimney, and he was working molten silver in a dish. May's father mistrusted him because he had neither land nor cattle and didn't care: under his forge-fire was buried silver, payment for weapons and tools and circumcisions, and he grinned through his dirty face, although the first smith bungled the first circumcision so the first man's son was an intersex and smiths are cursed.

3

Nothing happened about the bike, so Tom went back. He rode past the takeaway at closing time and crept behind parked cars to watch, his jacket over his head against the rain.

Big Chung was leaving. At the shop door he turned and waved through the plate glass, and with a shock Tom saw May behind the counter. 'She looks sad,' he thought. 'She's sad because her fat bastard father kicked me out.'

He ran after Chung, big but moving fast. 'Hey,' he said, trotting along, looking up. 'How you doing?'

'Yes.'

'I just wondered about May. If she was OK.'

'OK.'

'I really want to be friends with her.'

'Yes.'

'I mean I'm serious. I think she's . . . beautiful.'

'Cheerful girl,' said Chung, calm because unhittable.

'Beautiful.'

'Very cheerful.'

'But I get thrown out and May dumps me, just because I'm stoned. I mean, what happened? Why did you send me away?'

'Send?'

'OK. Why you give me my stuff, you and Wei?'

'Mr Tan don't like you.'

'Probably,' said Tom, pretending not to be hurt. 'But why May dumped me, why May not talk? Just because of dope, drugs, smoking?' and he mimed a joint.

'May don't like you.'

'No,' said Tom, trotting like a child. 'Not true. Or it's because of her dad, the racist shit. A racist shit, eh?' But Chung was too big to answer.

Tom said, 'Why you walk so fast?'

'Tired. Home.'

'God. You Chinese.'

Chung stared at him, then strode away: 'Tired. No Honda.'

Tom stood in the alley behind the takeaway. Next to Mr Tan's bedroom window was the pipe for the upstairs toilet. Further along, a drainpipe rose by Johnny's room. Between them was May's window, but there was no pipe to climb there.

Rain struck his face as he stared up, and he imagined May in a forest. They were slaves, but had run away because they weren't given salt. They'd found a good place, with the droppings of wild pig, fish in the river, and summer coming. He was looking up at the trees, which he would ringbark. They'd plant their crops in the fallen leaves.

Tom wiped a hand over his face. He looked for a light in May or Johnny's room, then limped down the alley. He was a mule-driver. He was leading a mule train through the mountains near Tibet, and May was a great lady under a silk umbrella. They'd halted in the snow and

10

he was boring a hole in a mule's throat, so it could breathe easier in the thin air. He winced on his crushed feet: mules had crippled him.

Tom came out onto the Whitechapel Road, his feet OK but now he was tired. He'd been following the plough, knee-deep in a flooded field, and he was leading the buffalo home to May. He had one buffalo but used to have two, which worked in harness for years. They wouldn't even drink at the river till they were properly aligned. But one of them broke into the granary and burst itself, so the other one thought that half the world had dropped away, or that it was walking by the edge of a cliff or a fast river, or the stable door was open or the stable wall had fallen, and it pulled the plough crooked. All day Tom had to hold the plough straight. He'd gripped the plough so hard that there was a flat bit on the gristle in his finger joints.

He scooped rain off the bike saddle. He revved the throttle, flexing his fingers, feeling the flat bit.

Back in Brixton, Tom plugged in the fire. He boiled a full kettle of water for the heat, then thought, 'I haven't washed since I got here.'

He carried the kettle up through the dark house, dodging water that dripped from the ceilings, the drips getting worse as he climbed so that it seemed like the roof was leaking. But Tom knew better. Last summer under the apple tree a hippy girl from down the terrace had said, 'People used to come here for baths, but now the water's cold.' He'd said, 'Let's fix it, then.'

They went upstairs, Tom admiring her wide soft arse and thinking, 'Afterwards we can go to my room.' The water tank was in a cupboard by the bathroom, and the job looked easy because the mains cable had come off the immersion heater. Tom said, 'But probably the fuse has gone,' and he touched the cable to the copper tank. There was a bang and the girl shrieked. Half blinded, Tom looked sideways at the scar on the copper. He laughed and said, 'Well, it's gone now.' Again he touched the tank with the cable end.

When his sight came back the girl had gone and a jet of water, bright as a new nail, was spouting from the side of the tank. It drooped smoothly downwards, wrinkling as it neared the floor, then pattered onto the floorboards and ran between his feet in dusty drops. Tom walked thoughtfully away, but afterwards he'd always stop on the landing below and look at the spreading stain on the ceiling. One day he came with a matchstick and chewing gum and plugged the leak, at least until he'd shut the cupboard door.

But he could see now that all through his time with May the water had been soaking down the stairwell, the ceilings falling floor by floor, wet plaster trodden into the landings. And he was edgy as he climbed in the dark because the cons kept their doors open. 'I suppose if you've been in a cell . . .'

He scowled into their rooms, just to show the buggers, most of them sat in the dark because of general bollock-brained incompetence, their ciggies glowing, a tinny radio somewhere. But then in the bathroom he was angry:

rubble in the bath, the toilet full of stuff you couldn't look at, and he was washing in a sink they probably pissed in. 'Dirty bastards.' He wouldn't wash again. Grease keeps you warm.

He was heading downstairs when someone shouted, 'Hey. The local yokel.' It was the red-headed Scouser, lounging in a room full of mattresses, a couple of other lowlifes smoking in the dark: 'You can bugger off out of that basement, pal. I'm having that room.'

Tom stamped down the stairs, kicking the fallen plaster, dodging under the hall ceiling that sagged and dripped, and splashing through the first pioneering drops that puddled outside his room. He lit a joint, then went to the basement steps and put his head back and shouted, 'Bollocks,' loud as he could up the stairwell. 'Bollocks, you ginger prat.'

He took off his wet pants and dried his legs on the curtain. He climbed into the doss bag and sat on the mattress in the red glow from the fire, feeling through the mattress the thump of trains along the Brixton viaduct, until the dope made everything fine. After a while he stopped shivering. He closed his eyes and thought about China. He was a fisherman on the river. He was old, so May had shortened his oars. He sat in the boat, angry and weeping.

Or he was mud-spattered. He was walking home, sick with tiredness. He opened the door and May looked up from pushing twigs into the stove. He smiled with anger. Every night he said the same thing. 'I stare at a buffalo's arse all day, but still you're ugly.'

Tom blinked awake. What was all that? Damn nasty dreams. Damn dope.

He told himself, 'May is my girl.' He closed his eyes and put himself back in China. Again he was by a river, waiting for May, his Chinese bride. She was dressing at her father's house. She had a tall hat. Tom saw the tiny brass discs on her skirt, and every stitch in her bridal shawl.

May turned to her father. Tom heard her, very clearly. 'I'm young and lovely, as you see. Give me a potion to remain so.'

Her father said, 'Drink this and you'll live for ever.'

May drank, then clutched her stomach.

Her father said, 'Did you eat meat today?'

'At the marriage breakfast, of course.'

'Fool! The potion has brought it back to life.'

May rolled on the ground, saying, 'The beef has horns. The pork has sharp teeth.'

May's father carried her from the house. He laid her body at Tom's feet, then danced down the riverbank, singing, 'She's young and lovely, as you see.'

4

Tom watched the hospital. Light from the double doors spilled over the wet forecourt and the turning ambulances. He came slowly to the stone porch, and inside onto squeaky green lino. And here was lanky Frank, the Aussie doctor, saying, 'Hey. How's your dick?'

'I'm looking for May.'

'She's not on tonight.'

'No? You're not lying, are you, Frank?'

'Also, we don't actually do social calls.'

'Well, my head's a bit buggered,' said Tom. 'Too much dope, I think.'

'Seen your GP?'

'I thought you were maybe very clever, so probably you'd have an antidote.'

''Fraid not,' said Frank.

'Look, you clown, I just want to see her.'

Frank stared down at him, which seemed pretty bold for such a long streak of nothing. He flapped his hand: 'You're welcome to wait.' Plastic chairs full of the glum and drunk.

'Christ. I'll leave a note, then.'

Tom was patting his jacket so Frank gave him a biro and then, sighing, found a form headed 'To be completed before admission'. Tom looked dumb so the Aussie said, 'On the other side, OK?'

Tom said, 'Frank, did you know you're going bald at the back?'

He sat in the waiting room, thinking he'd been weak with that long Aussie bastard, even picking up his accent. Should have punched him after that 'How's your dick' thing, which was a wind-up.

On his first night with May they'd kissed on the bed and she was rolling around on top of him and then his pants were sticky. He went to the bathroom and he was plastered in blood. He thought it must be her period, but then he took his pants down. He ran back to her in a panic, saying, 'My cock has burst.' They climbed on the bike and she took him to A&E and laughed when Doctor Frank called it 'a nosebleed in your dick'. They waited a week, and then another week because she was on nights, and then she had incense in her room and a red cloth over the bedside light and new panties. He didn't say that it was his first time.

He also didn't mention his foreskin. It had always been tight, a twoskin maybe, and he'd never understood its workings till they did it in biology. For years he tried forcing it back, but this left white stretch marks, which were scar tissue and made it tighter. He entered her and yelped.

He pulled back and lay bewildered, May saying, 'OK?' He went to the bathroom and his foreskin was stuck back. She watched as he got dressed, but he only said, 'I have to go.' Eventually she was quiet. Maybe it was her first time as well. Again he climbed carefully onto the bike and buzzed through dark streets to A&E, but this time he sat for hours. He could feel his knob end. It chafed against his clothes, raw as an eyeball, but its messages came from somewhere unplaceable. Occasionally he checked in the toilet, his foreskin still stuck, a bit of blood, and his plum going black. Then Doctor Frank again, who was impressed: 'Hey, it's strangulated.' By morning Tom was circumcised.

He woke slowly after the operation. He stared out the window, then lifted the sheet. A full English breakfast. Then the stitches got infected, so he read May's China books for a month, horny with someone else's dick, till she lit candles around the bath and they drank wine among the bubbles while her dad rattled the door and went away muttering.

'We could try tomorrow,' she said. But they couldn't because she was drunk and then the two cooks took him to play pool and the next night he was dumped.

So now he was back in the hot waiting room, twiddling the biro, hoping she'd walk past. He wrote: 'Hello baby I miss you, if you want you can contact me at the following address 1 Canterbury Crescent (The Basement) Brixton or anywhere you like, I really miss you!'

He looked round for Frank, then drifted down the corridor and turned a corner. He had to lean against the wall. There was May, writing something in a glass-walled office.

He went forward. Still she didn't see. He touched the doorframe, the wood blurred with overpainting. How sad and kind and cute she looked.

'Get out,' she said, turning away. 'Get out, get out.'

He put the note on the table, not looking at her. 'Please, May. I mean—'

Behind him the Aussie said, 'Can I help you?'

'Yes. Fuck off.' He said to May, 'Your dad. Just because I was stoned. Don't listen to him, May. Please.'

But there were wiry brown arms round his waist, Tom shouting, 'Bastard,' and bracing his heels. The doctor carried him towards the office door, creepy long bones keeping him easily off the lino.

But the door was narrow and Tom got his feet either side of the frame, saying, 'You see,' skinny Frank twisting and pushing and getting tired.

May ducked through the doorway. She stood between Tom's feet with her head tipped, like you might threaten a child. She held the rolled-up note like a club.

'Please,' said Tom.

But she made a pretend flick at his bollocks and at once Frank was carrying him to the street door, Tom hitting backwards with his head and heels but not connecting.

Down the sides of the corridor were big notice boards, green baize under glass. He thought, 'That's dangerous in a hospital,' then punched the glass.

He held up his hand, saying, 'Look, you shit. Now you can't throw me out.'

He got back to the squat at 1 a.m., his hand throbbing from working the throttle, the bandage very white as he went down the dark stairs to the basement. His light was on, the Scouse drunk sitting on his mattress saying, 'It's the country boy.'

Tom stared at him, and at first the Scouser laughed at Tom's comedy eyebrows. But finally he shrugged and stood up slowly. He stretched and said, 'Nice room, pal.'

He walked casually past, Tom stepping out of range then giving him a huge kick in the arse, booting him out of the room and into the far wall.

Tom watched him through the shouting. When he'd gone Tom sat down and lit a spliff, the mattress warm from the shit-clagged red-haired bum on that Scouse git, who'd said, 'You don't belong here,' and, 'Wait till you're asleep.'

Tom slid into the doss bag, the light still on, wincing when he pulled his stitches, put in by a cute lady doctor at the outside clinic where Doctor Frank had sent him by ambulance, a security guard for company. The guard had watched them with folded arms, but the doctor was still kind, though not Chinese.

'May, where are you?' He rolled over and closed his eyes, so she could come to him in China.

He was tired. He was standing by a river. Long ago he'd been married here with May Tan. Now it was night and he was talking to May's father, and May was dead.

He said, 'Why did you call me here?'

Her father said, 'May is haunting me.'

Now there was a sobbing from the far bank. 'Every night,' said her father. 'Every night.'

Tom thought, 'In this country, a ghost can drag men to her grave.' He stared across the dark river and said, 'She's angry because you drove me away.'

'You're trembling,' said the father. 'Coward! That's why I drove you away.'

'And so she killed herself. Talk to her. She wants a reckoning.'

The father went to his boat. Bitterly he said, 'Why didn't you fight for her?'

Tom stood on the riverbank, watching the little boat in the moonlight. It came to the middle of the river. He heard the father call, 'May, he's come.' Then he heard a sob behind him.

5

Tom was still asleep when Wei and Chung came round. He sat on the mattress, rubbing his face, groggy from the dream.

'Tea?' he said, and pulled on his shoes. He went to the toilet and dipped the kettle in the cistern, little Wei poking his head around the door, laughing and saying, 'Whaaat?'

'It's clean water. Anyway, I boil, so . . .'

'Smelly here!'

'Free tea, all right?'

'Why you live here?' said Wei. 'Crazy!'

'No job, remember.'

'Ah, no job. Maybe your fault.'

Tom said, 'How you find me? This house, how?'

'You told May.'

'Christ.'

Wei passed him a scrap of paper. It was the corner of a Chinese newspaper, a name and number scrawled in the margin. Tom said, 'Who's Ellie?'

'Your father's friend. May says: Tom call Ellie.'

'OK. Tell her thanks.' He was touched. 'Tell her that's very kind. Or I'll tell her, actually.'

Wei laughed. 'No, no. Not kind. Don't talk to her, all right? She said don't call, don't talk.'

Tom was silenced, making the tea: 'You share, OK?'

'One cup!' said Wei, squatting and grinning. Big Chung leaned on the wall, his look saying, 'What do you expect from this fool?' as Tom irritably took the bandage off his hand, checked the stitches and threw the bloody bandage in a corner. 'All right, Chung, you thick prick, how's work?'

'Johnny dead.'

'What?' Chung didn't answer, so Tom sat with his eyes wide until Wei sighed and said, 'Maybe we get the bike. Key, please.'

Tom rinsed the cup in the cistern, Wei saying, 'My god.' He put the tea-making kit in a supermarket bag and hung it on a nail behind the curtain. The electric fire went under a torn rug below the basement steps.

'Really?' said Tom. 'He's really dead?' They didn't answer so he thought, 'Bollocks to this. Bollocks and porrocks.'

He said, 'Hang on,' and went into the toilet and closed the door. There was an old painted-over bolt that nobody used. He pushed it quietly but it was only half home when there was a shout and a great thump on the door. He was climbing out of the toilet window when Chung grabbed his ankle. He kicked him off and scrambled over the wall into the next garden and out to the street.

Still raining. He jumped on the wet saddle and teetered away, big Chung gaining on him, Wei on the pavement laughing. He screwed up the throttle, his hand sore, Chung left behind in the blue exhaust.

*

'A moped? I can't do nothing with a moped.'

'I just want something that drives. For old times' sake.' Tom was at Bert the Breaker's, avenues of wrecks stretching off around them. 'Look, you dick. Anything, OK.'

Bert held up his hands: 'Relax.' He looked again at the Honda, red and new. 'Well, there's this little van.'

'A van,' said Tom. 'Great.' He thought, 'I'm crap at bargaining.'

'Down there. On the right, near the bus. Ex Post Office. Very practical.'

'I've never had a van,' said Tom. 'Can you sleep in it?'

'What do you mean "sreep"?'

'Sleep, then.'

'Definitely.'

Tom stepped around rainbow puddles, the bare earth black with oil, cars piggybacked in the rain. Crappy England. The van was low and dented and green, painted with a brush over the Post Office red. The back doors groaned when he opened them, his hands blue from the long ride out of London.

'I've never had a van.' He could park at night and creep in the back, curled up asleep while people walked past. He leaned on the doors to shut them. Half a tank of juice, although the dipstick was low. But you can always get oil, he thought, if you don't mind crawling under cars with a wrench – which, on the other hand, he didn't actually have.

The gears crunched on the way back to Brixton, but he thought, 'I won't be driving much.' The smell of new wire, threads of copper in the footwell, a cardboard roll of mains cable sliding around the back, and the pleasure of a junk car, jostling the traffic, nothing to lose. My van. Though the heater didn't work.

He crept round the back of the squat and peeked through his window. No one. He went in through the toilet window and dragged his mattress out of the front door to the street. He leaned his folded arms on the roof, catching his breath, then stuffed the mattress in the back of the van. It curled up the sides and pushed against the back doors, so he went behind the squat, opening his knife, and cut the washing line off the apple tree. He closed the back doors of the van against the mattress, tying their handles together with the line.

The van would slope into the gutter when he parked up, and he could roll into the trough of the mattress and be hidden and safe. 'This good.'

He rolled the rest of his stuff into the rug and dumped it in the van with that fine feeling of leaving. He'd tried to favour his cut hand, but there were dabs of blood on the mattress and the rug and all over the van. He sat in the driver's seat, taking a breather with the door open, Londoners tramping past, doing whatever they did.

He was sleepy, as always. He drove to a side street, crashing the rubbish gears, and parked up, thinking how you could have some kind of selective-breeding thing. You'd pick the sallow and squinty types, till everyone was Chinese.

He climbed in the back of the van and laid out the doss bag. Too much light from the front, so he fixed the curtain behind the seats, tying it with scraps of wire to the seatbelt mountings. He sat on the mattress, pulling bits of prickly copper thread from his socks. He took off his shoes and lay down.

What about Johnny? Maybe some Chinky thing where 'dead' means 'dead to us'. Into the doss bag, fully clothed. He lit his last spliff and his bones eased.

The van rocked as a bus went past. He covered himself with the curtain and rug. The traffic was loud. He'd get earplugs. He squirmed deeper into the doss bag, but there was still a draught on his face, very cold. It smelled of the river. He saw a wooden house on a riverbank.

'Not again.'

He lived in the little wooden house. He slept on rice straw, which pricked his ankles. He picked rice grains from the straw because his father starved him. On a wall by his bed was a picture of a girl. His father had made the picture, murmuring certain words over the paints, so that every night the girl stepped down from the picture and cooked and cleaned and returned to the picture at dawn. The old man called her 'daughter', but the boy said nothing because he was shy.

Now night was falling. His father said, 'From tonight you'll sleep in the stable.'

The boy went to the stable and lay beside the little pony, which sighed and stamped. He was too angry to sleep. He went back across the yard and crept to a window and saw his father naked with the girl. 'I'll call you May,' the old man said, 'because you are young.'

The boy went to the picture and tore it with his sharp nails. His father screamed all night, because the girl gripped him with her torn flesh.

In the morning the old man burnt the picture. His son took the pony and went downstream to find his fortune, although the old man begged him to stay. But no one would come to the lonely house by the river. Every night the old man was sickened by ghostly kisses, which tasted of burnt skin.

6

Tom felt well hidden in the van in the dark in the rain in the Jack-the-Ripper alley behind the takeaway. Nine o'clock. He was watching for May going to or from her baffling shifts, because the dreams meant that her dad was to blame. 'Listen to me,' he'd say. 'Not that fat rat.'

And he'd ask about Johnny. No wonder she was upset. 'Take your time. Really. I'll be here when you're ready.' White scalp at her parting, the separate hairs, and how with her hand flat she rubbed her lovely snub nose.

'Damn.' Instead of May it was little Wei, stepping out for a smoke. Tom watched him drop the lighter, pick it up, then pout his fag into the flame, cross-eyed and cautious like a child. 'Wei!'

Walking crooked under the rain, head tipped, Wei came over. Comedy recognition: 'Ah! You!'

'Not so loud!' The van window was stuck halfway, Tom squinting up through the gap. 'Hurry up, will you. Get in.'

Wei stared, his clothes on crooked like a child or a corpse, then squeezed along the wet wall in the dark and into the passenger seat. His shrivelled jockey face. 'Tom! You are well?'

'Yes, thank you.'

'You work now?'

'No. In fact I wanted to know why I got the sack. Why I lost the job, the work, the bike.'

'Ah! Bike! Where, Tom?'

'I gave it back. Mr Tan has it. Or he will soon anyway. Look, forget the bike.'

'OK,' said Wei cheerfully.

'I just wondered how is May. And Mr Tan.'

'Very sad about Johnny. And May, very sad.'

'He die? Really? How?'

'I don't know, Tom.'

'What you mean, you don't know? That's crap.'

Startled, Wei said, 'Kill himself.'

Tom thought, 'I'm not ready for this.' He said, 'Got a ciggie?'

'Your father's friend – you phone?'

'Forget my damn dad.' Tom sucking down smoke. Fantastic. And bollocks to Wei and Mr Tan and all of them except May. Then he said, 'Bugger!'

'Bugger!' said Wei, and they leant right back because May was at the kitchen door, looking round.

Tom said, 'Did she see us?'

'Maybe no. Night.'

'I have to go.'

'Wait, wait. I work.'

'I'm going.'

'No, no. I work.'

'Hang on,' said Tom. 'Wait. Just slide out quietly. Understand? Get out of your side. She can't see that side. Just get out very, very quietly.'

'I get out,' said Wei, softly opening the door.

They'd forgotten the courtesy light. Illuminated, they sat stunned. Then Wei tumbled out as the van raced off, May watching astonished as Tom crashed the gears and said, 'Bugger,' because now the van was useless for stakeouts.

A mile down the road he stamped on the brakes and cut into a side street. He got out and walked around the van, kicking tyres, picking at rust, stroking dents in the passenger door, which Wei hadn't shut so that it hit parked cars all along the Whitechapel Road.

Poor Johnny. Poor May. Because of their bastard dad.

He climbed in the back and lay down. Boring, being homeless. Too angry to sleep, he didn't get into the doss bag. Damn cold, though, so he pulled it over him.

He remembered dozing in May's room, her China books sharing the bed, until at dawn she crept in beside him. Silent and happy, he'd hear the pigeons stirring on the roof, their claws on the slates, their foolish cooing like his own wonder. Or if she was on days he'd roam through London, so at ease that he'd smile at women and they smiled right back. But now he stank of failure, scared of May, stupid with loss.

He closed his eyes and at once tasted dust. He was lying on his face. It was night, and very cold. He was lying on the ground, the dust in his mouth. At the same time, though, he could see himself from above, so that he was in the dream but also watching it.

'No more dreams.'

He saw May. She was leaving a wooden house and crossing a yard. She stopped, because someone was lying by the latrine.

She screamed, and a boy ran from the house.

Tom thought, 'It's her brother.'

May raised her lamp over the stranger. The lamplight showed a terrible wound. When the brother saw the wound he thought, 'So this is how women are.' When May saw the entrails she thought, 'So this is how men are.'

The brother carried the stranger to an empty room, and afterwards paced alone. At midnight he went to the stranger and stammered his love, then slipped into the bed. May was modest, waiting till dawn before she went to the stranger's room.

They went to the stranger every midnight and every dawn, each creeping in secret through the house. And their love put a false life into the stranger, so that the ghost couldn't get free of the body. Often the ghost drifted towards the river, which is the route to the afterworld, wondering if it was alive or dead and if it was man or woman. But it was always called back by the false life in the body. When the ghost returned, the body could open its eyes and sit up and say yes and no, though often in the wrong place.

Every night the brother stayed later and the sister arrived sooner. At last they met in the stranger's room. They were ashamed and angry, and May raged at her lover's deceit. Without their love the body died, and they burned it behind the house and threw its ashes in the river.

But this was too late for the ghost, which pines for their love. On windy nights it howls and on rainy nights it taps on the door. Inside, the brother and sister embrace while the night howls and taps.

Tom woke with a jolt.

Damn dreams are getting longer. He'll endure them, though. He'll follow them through every possible world, because they're about May.

On the other hand they're horrible. 'No more dope, anyway.'

He lay in the back of the van as night rain clattered on the roof. Poor Johnny.

Stiff and cold, he climbed slowly over the seats and sat behind the wheel. He got out and stretched, still druggy from the dream.

Eleven o'clock. Cold rain, so he got back in and watched women coming past, reeling and laughing from the pub, their fate on their face like the number on a bus. But there were too many tight jeans, the bollocklessness, so he started the van and drove.

Out of habit he went to Brixton, angry with himself. 'Not the squat again.' He parked and slammed the door and stalked down the Crescent, stiff with rage: Johnny and May, both messed up by their bastard dad.

People milling around a squat, and he went in for the pleasure of pushing through. Along the hall and down the basement steps and into a roar of noise. No music, but a bellowing crowd swayed in the dark, and there was cold around his ankles like water or a draught.

The red-headed drunk pushed past, Tom saying, 'Hello, wanker,' angry and pleased.

'Oh, the farm boy.' He waved a spliff, laughing, close enough to knee him. 'We didn't frighten you away, did we?'

'I've got my own place now.'

'Excellent room. Ta very much. Very kind.'

'Central heating,' said Tom. 'Everything. And I'm sharing with a girl. Chinese.' But the Scouser had gone away laughing.

The dripping ceiling bulged down, and he was squashed against a circle of men, who grinned and raised their plastic glasses. In the middle was a girl. A man spat in his beer and gave it her. 'I don't mind,' she said, and drank. Somebody snatched the glass and put his dick in the beer. 'I don't mind,' she said, Tom pushing away but finding the redhead again, lounging with his pals against a corner, his hands cupped round his mouth: 'Don't be scared, farm boy.'

Tom aimed for the door but a girl grabbed his arm, saying, 'I know you.' Square hands, a dancer's stocky body: 'I saw you. Last year. You fix cars. You fix cars so you can fix my bike, OK?' Bad hippy teeth, bleached moustache, a ribbon with glitter in her dirty-blonde hair. She pulled his sleeve. 'Hello? Anybody there? My bike. Understand? You speak English?'

Tom said, 'Um.'

'Can't hear you.'

He hated to shout over the noise. He cleared his throat and said, 'Chinese.'

His village: mud around the well, the dirt track that twists and lifts from the riverbank – unchanging things.

She looked at him crooked, a little nervous laugh, finger-shaped bruises on her bare arms. 'You're never Chinese.'

'Well . . .' He was a Whitechapel tailor. Fifty years over a steam iron, too bent to see the photo on the shelf: his sons, their children and children's children, in the middle his child bride, also old, in the village with the track rising from the river.

'You mean you were born in China?' Her face twisted, trying to believe. 'I mean you're not Chinese.'

'A particular tribe in China. We're a bit . . .' Couldn't finish the thought.

'White?' she said, laughing.

The village road was a blacktop now, but he'd always know the lift and half-turn up from the river, passing the well, capped now with a concrete slab, with a steel box where an engine thumped an hour a day, filling a tank above the village so that the houses had taps, and the old and the young would press their hands on the pipe to feel the engine, and the only mud was a hand-sized patch where a pipe-joint leaked. His bones would be carried up the bend and past the well, home after fifty years.

He thought, 'But who puts a well by a river?'

'Let's go, let's go,' he told the girl. 'This is disgusting.'

She paused, but the redhead shouted, 'Smell his cock first. All sheep-shitty.' The girl frowned and led him towards the door, Tom murmuring under the din: 'The river was dirty.' He saw a concrete town, a rusted outflow pipe squirting milky liquid into the river, paper snagged on a midstream branch, and a pale smear on the water, coiling downstream to the village. He said, 'The river was dirty, so we dug a well.'

Into the back yard, tripping on bricks and beer cans. 'It's really raining,' she said, but he couldn't answer. 'Is that your village? I mean, with the well. You're talking about China, right?' But he wouldn't speak English.

'Deaf again,' she said, hunched against the rain. 'Christ. Come on.'

He followed her down the back of the terrace, her strong waist, rain drifting from the dark, the gardens clearer of junk as they got to the hippy end.

In through a back door and into a living room with collapsed comfortable sofas, Afghan mats, swirly paintings, purple skirting boards – stuff that Number One had been drifting towards before the crackheads came, and then the cons who threw them out.

Downstairs to the basement kitchen. A big pine table, at the sink a good-looking man, paint flecks on his overalls. 'Hey, Annie. Hey, man. Hey, I know you!' Pushing long brown hair behind his ears. 'Last year, right? I used to see you, with the cars.' He laughed: 'You always looked, I don't know – surprised.'

'Don't you worry about flooding?' said Tom. 'I mean in a basement.'

The man laughed again, handsome and happy: 'Seriously?'

'I don't know. Maybe.'

'I hadn't thought about it. You think we should?'

A silence until the girl said, 'He goes deaf on you.'

Mr Handsome gave him a wobbly homemade cup with no handle. 'Soothing, man.' Tea with petals and bits. 'A mechanic, right? I can't do engines. Too . . . something.' He grinned, forgiving himself. 'But we need a mechanic, definitely.'

'He's from China, he says. He talks like Farmer Giles but really he's Chinese.'

'Wow. Really? Which part? I went to the south. Only three months, though. Travelled around, off the tourist trail. Amazing place. You mean you're actually from there?'

Tom staring at the table, the fancy tea in a homemade cup, fingerprints in the clay. 'Hippy shit.'

'Sorry, man?'

'All this hippy shit.' A kitty and a cleaning rota. A communal pushbike. All that cooler-than-thou crap.

'You like that other stuff, then, up the terrace?' said the girl. Tom thought: You don't belong either – finger bruises, a glittery ribbon, satin slippers with the ballerina straps, and just a bit too old.

'See? He goes deaf on you.' If I had a gun. Knives in the kitchen drawer. 'No answer. We're not worth talking to, I suppose.'

Tom went to the kitchen door and struggled with the bolt, his stitches sore, then out into the dark, the girl saying, 'Oops. Off he goes. Back to China.'

He climbed across a tumbled wall into the next garden, falling over a supermarket trolley, the girl shouting, 'Bye-bye, China boy.'

He groped forward and found a house wall and followed it in the dark, trailing his hand along the wet bricks, climbing over rubble and a broken fence and out to the street. His little van, patient in the rain.

He checked the line on the back doors, leaned for a while on the bonnet, then sat in the driver's seat, slumped over with weariness. He was bent-backed. It was his own fault. 'Eat the bones,' his father always said. But the fish bones pricked his mouth so he secretly palmed them and put his hand on the bamboo floor and pushed them through the gaps to the river below. It was easy to palm them because everyone ate with their hands. But now he couldn't straighten to see the picture on the shelf, his sons and great-grandsons and his child bride with an old face.

7

Tom was asleep in the van. He grunted and squirmed, watching a man in a little wooden town by a river.

It was all very clear – the man with a baby on his back, the dusty streets of the town, and the river grey and fast, with boats pulled up on the bank.

'His wife is dead,' thought Tom.

He watched the man walk slowly like a rustic, till he came to a low hut on the riverbank. Nearby was a pile of fish heads and fish bones which stank even in this cold air, a crow treading its summit. He waited outside the low door, looking up and down the river, until a fat little pig came trotting around the hut. It sniffed towards him, alert and interested, pulling against the rope through its earflap. At this the man ducked inside. It was very dark. After a while he saw a fire and something shiny. It was the silver tooth of an old woman, who grinned and said, 'Your honour?'

The man had rehearsed his speech: 'Find me a wife who'll care for me and my house and my baby girl.' He pushed a coin into the old woman's hand and she smiled again: the man's clothes were ragged and the coin was tarnished from long burial under his hearth fire. And she thought how a baby girl is a curse, because she must be fed until she's ready to work, but then goes to her husband's house so that her parents grow old alone. She put the money into her clothes and forgot the matter.

For months the man waited in his little house in the hills, with its one field whose best crop was stones, which rose to the surface after every rain or every ploughing. He was too ashamed to go back to the town, so at last he walked far upstream, his daughter heavier on his back, lying down for the night behind a boulder in a high pass, his daughter fretful. On the second day he came to a larger town and another marriage broker.

This time, though, he had dressed his daughter as a boy. 'A plump son,' he told the broker, 'who'll bring a woman and children to my house, to care for me and the fortunate wife you will find.' But he had no money and gave the broker a poor brass necklace that his dead wife had worn. The old woman sneered as she tucked the necklace into her boot, and at once forgot the matter.

Again the man waited in the hills, gathering his daily harvest of stones. As he waited he kept the girl in boy's clothes, although there was no one to see except the beggars that he drove from his gate and the travelling salt-vendors.

He was proud to have a son. They joked and raced and had spitting games and threw a ball of rags across his stony field, so that the child laughed and clapped her hands. She grew lean and brown like a boy, though once he found her cradling the ball of rags and crooning, so he beat her. And he beat her if she bathed or tidied the house or washed her clothes or combed her hair. Her name was May, but he only said, 'Good boy,' and 'My son.'

And he banished animals from the farm, in case she saw the difference in male and female, only keeping chickens, where the male parts are hidden. And likewise they ate lizards and snakes, and collected eggs from the nests of ground-dwelling birds. A wild dog attacked the chickens and his daughter killed it and said, 'What are those parts?'

'A big worm and a big tick,' he said, 'that sucked its blood.'

Another time she said, 'Father, why do I sit to pee but you stand up?'

'You've crouched because you were young, but now you can wear a peeing part.' And he made her an earthenware spout, and made one for himself, which he pretended to use.

And finally she said, 'Why am I bleeding?'

'Because now you're a man. Your blood can mix with a woman's blood to make babies.' Alone, he rubbed his hands and said, 'I'll find her a wife.'

He went to a third marriage broker and the search was easy. He ignored the talk of beauty or wealth and chose an idiot girl, who'd been raised by aunts and toiled all day like a beast. The wedding was a hurried thing and the aunts were not invited. Afterwards he gave his daughter a carved thighbone. 'This is called a wedding part,' he said.

Now the farm had another worker, though he mocked the idiot wife, saying, 'Look how she spills the water, which you carried so far.' But his daughter was happy, and the wife smiled so that she was almost pretty.

The father was glad that his daughter wasn't used by

a man. But he was jealous of the women, who laughed as they cleared a second field, and whispered at the day's end, perhaps thinking of the wedding part. The women kept it in their bed. It was tied with a silk ribbon and lay in a silk sleeve which the wife had made.

One day the man lifted a stone and hurt his back. It wasn't a big stone, and he lay in the house drinking barley beer and thinking that now he was old. He remembered the games with his daughter and thought how he'd never have a grandson. That night he woke up choking because he smelled the women or because their breath had drained the air.

Next day he lay drunk in bed while the idiot wife bustled about the house and his daughter trimmed maize in the yard. He said, 'Where is the wedding part?'

The wife stared at him.

'Where is the wedding part that I made?'

She looked towards the window.

'Did you think that your husband made it?' said the father, laughing. 'No, it was me. And now I'll burn it.'

'No,' said the idiot wife.

'I'll burn it because I have a special wedding part. Do you want to see it?'

'No.'

'It's a special wedding part that makes babies. Do you want babies?'

The idiot wife thought about this.

'You want babies, of course. Come here. Look at my special wedding part.'

When the wife came he pulled her onto the bed. His

back hurt, and he was surprised at her strength, or perhaps at his own weakness. But he pressed on, the wife shouting under him until his daughter came running with the shears.

She chopped off his special wedding part and he bled to death.

As he died he told them how to fix the roof, about men and women, and where to buy goats, which would prosper on these stony hills. The women were puzzled. That winter, though, the wife had his child.

It was a boy, so now the women understood. They were happy together and their son grew fat. In time he married and had many sons, who played in the stony fields, and ran with the goats, and cared for the two grandmammas when they were old.

Tom woke in the dark. He was shivering in the driver's seat, thinking that maybe dicks are full of gristle and hard to cut, especially with farm shears. And wouldn't your dick shrink if someone came at you with shears? Or you'd fight them off, surely, even if you were drunk. And would you really bleed to death? So maybe the dream couldn't be true.

'Forget the dream.' But unknowingly he touched his pants because they might be bloody.

He fired up the van and set off anywhere. 'I'm in China more than I'm here.' A new thumping from the van, the gear stick shuddering so that it blurred.

Then he thought, 'Saturday night,' and went round the Elephant and Castle double-yolker roundabouts and turned north. On King's Cross Road he parked up and crossed to the pool hall. He straightened for the door-cam and flashed his membership card. An inordinate pause until the lock buzzed.

He bounded up the stairs feeling glad, and here's that wonder – an all-night bar. 'Good evening, gents,' he said, bowing through the gloom to the slackers on the red plush benches. 'What a place, eh?'

An old barman, shaky and slow, and Tom said, 'Lager, please, pal,' and checked his pockets. 'Shit. Just a half, actually,' the alky barman confused, then careful with the glasses like he's on a boat.

Embarrassed, Tom drifted to the big windows on to the snooker room. 'I should pick up my dole.' He put his nose to the thick glass. Rows of tables dwindling into the gloom, a library hush, and men bent to play or leaning like sentries with spears. He turned to the nearest drinkers and lifted his childish glass: 'Gentlemen, the great London secret. And it took a bunch of Chinese to show me.'

But then he said, 'Damn,' because he saw the black Doc Martens shoes, black official polyester trousers. 'Coppers, eh?'

'Never,' said one. 'In an after-hours bar?' Neat hair, well-filled sleeves.

'Well, right. And tragic if it got shut down.'

'You on something?' said a cop, young and therefore dangerous. 'You on the naughty substances?'

'Just a natural high.' Tom said, 'Could I? Do you mind if . . . ?' and he's wiggling a cigarette out of a pack on the table.

The young cop nodded: 'Natural.'

'Certainly. Just happy to see you gents enjoy your-self. Yes. Among the common folk. And I wish you well. Really I do. Slumming.' A stillness settled through the cops at this, watching more than listening, so that Tom said quickly, 'Well, must be going. Enjoy. Enjoy your-selves. Really. I really really mean that.' Jesus, shut up.

Sweating, he aimed for the basement because the Chi-nese prefer pool. Metal-edged stairs that make your bones ache, then out into the strip-lit pool room. 'Dead China-men,' he thought, because big Chung loomed among the Chinatown cooks, and all of them yellow-brown under the lights. They love strip lights. Drives away demons maybe or something. Like in the Tan kitchen after hours, the leftovers shiny in a surgical glare.

He sat on a crooked chair against the wall, hidden behind the fag machine, watching Chung practise alone. Where was that little rat Wei? But maybe I can get more sense out of Chung, who's big and calm or big and stupid. He slid the unlit cigarette into a pocket and strode out under the merciless light.

'Hello, Chung.'

'Yes.' Glancing round, baffled.

'How are you?'

'Yes.'

Tom patting his jacket. 'Look, you got a smoke?' Chung sighed, taking his time to haul out the Marlboros, Tom twitching. 'Chung, I want to ask you something. About Johnny.'

'Johnny suicide.'

'Yes, yes. We know this.'

'Johnny suicide because you.'

'What? That's crap.' Chung frowning, beer glass in his huge hand. Why does he hate me? Tom sucked down the smoke. 'God, that's good. Jesus. Anyway. I wondered, Chung. Leaving aside your usual shite. I mean, OK I was stoned that night. But this is not very bad. So then what? I lose job because Johnny dead? Why? Why, please?'

'Johnny dead because you. And because you friend from hospital.'

'Hospital?'

'Old people hospital. You and friends and Johnny.'

Dread in his belly, and Chung's angry face, big as a bum.

Tom said, 'God, this place. Bad lights, bad chairs. Why upstairs so nice? Because upstairs bloody white people maybe.'

'Forget,' said Chung. He was giving Tom the straight look, looming over him, Tom looking up at the black-heads in Chung's flat nose in his flat face, his fingers spread on Tom's chest, pressing a warning. 'Forget May. Forget takeaway. Don't come. Never.'

'I can't forget. Damn dreams.'

Chung tramped off for a closer look at a clutch of balls, Tom looking round the room, alone and stupid. He swallowed. Johnny and the old folks' home, and now the sick dread.

Abruptly he ran up the stairs, and there were the cops again.

'Hi. Hello, lads.' Their blank stare, and Tom breathless. 'I wondered maybe if you could help. It's a friend of mine. He's dead. A couple of weeks back. Very unexpected. So I wondered, when's the inquest, do you reckon?'

An old copper said, 'Depends. But probably it's been and gone.'

'Well, I want to object. I've got evidence. They're saying suicide, but he was murdered. As good as.'

'Best tell the police, then.'

'Well, for fuck's sake I'm telling you.'

'Yes, but we're not here.'

'Bollocks,' said Tom, flustered. 'Smart crap.'

The cop decided to be kind. 'Listen, son. A word of advice.'

'Fuck off,' said Tom, and at last had the sense to leave.

8

Towards dawn he was sleepy in the van near Blackfriars
Bridge, blinking across the river at birds like flags over
the office blocks. But he hated daylight so he climbed over
the seats and under the curtain, his eyes mostly closed,
finding the doss bag by touch, then curling up tight so
that he didn't think about the coppers and big Chung and
'you friend from hospital'.

'I'll think about the river.'

It was grey and fast. It ran by Chelsea and the Isle of
Dogs. But first it flowed under houses on stilts, and past a
dirty fishing town, and swiftly below a black cliff, sheer
as a building.

'Bastards. All of them.'

He stared hard at the cliff. There was a tiny house. It
clung to the cliff face. It was called a 'sky farm', because
its fields were scraps of land on ledges and crannies in the
terrible rock.

He saw the farmer. On ropes of woven bamboo, and
on bamboo pegs wedged in the black rock, he climbed to
fields as small as rugs, which he covered with flat stones
to keep the soil moist and save it from the fretting cliff-
top winds.

'Beautiful,' said Tom. 'Oh, beautiful.'

The house was half on a ledge and half on beams

46

driven into the cliff. Below, the rock fell sheer to the river. Above, it rose to a meadow on the cliff top, where wiry grass was nibbled by goats. The goatherds dropped stones on the little family, to keep them in their station, and the goats climbed down and ate their crops.

Tom saw the farmer's wife. She was calling and calling from the house door. The farmer didn't answer. She looked across the cliff face and put her hand to her mouth. There were two broken pegs – one which had snapped beneath him, and one he had broken as he fell to the river.

'God,' thought Tom.

So now the woman worked alone. She crept in terror to the scraps of land, her son and daughter playing by the house, ropes around their waist to keep them from the edge where the tiny garden stepped into air. They were twins, and wore their mother's cast-off clothes, so that even she was confused.

The little boy hated to climb, but his twin, free of male entanglements, was soon busy on the cliff, her fingers sure as roots in the cracks of the handholds. Their mother watched from the garden, holding the little boy, who shouted, 'May!'

Around their house were the lovely plants of the heights – azaleas, mauve primulas, maidenhair fern, palm trees, golden and green bamboo, clematis, white and yellow roses – springing from cracks which the father hadn't reached. But May crept to the plants, cutting them for kindling and pushing the seedling of an orange or pomelo into the cupful of earth, looking straight down between her feet to the tiny boats on the river, and the riverside town, its folk too small to see.

Asleep, Tom held his breath. He was watching May, beautiful and brave on the cliff face.

Her mother ceased to work. Angry in her fear, she said, 'May is the farmer and I am a useless extra mouth.' She went to the riverside town and came home smelling of drink and the hands of river coolies. One day her son watched amazed as she folded her clothes at the edge of the garden and stood naked, then followed her husband into the river.

So May kept the house. She found new fields, little as pillows on the black cliff, and knelt on the spongy new earth, looming like a moon over the wiry grass and the flowers like trees in this small world, and perhaps a household of ants and a spider brought by the wind. She tore off the turf like a scab and turned it over and weighted it with stones and planted her crops, so that there was food to sell, and salt twice a week.

Now certain stirrings began. On hot nights she stood at the cliff edge, the night wind strong up her shift then weak where it tickled her breasts, and thought how the townsfolk might see up her shift, though they were too far down. And in the daytime she watched the town from a scrap of tilted earth, until perhaps a river bird rose with stiff wings up the cliff, and saw her with a squawk, and drifted out over the river. She had no mirror, and remembered her mother, who perhaps had wondered if she was pretty enough to fly.

Like his sister, the boy heard the rustle of wings. But it

seemed like the rustle of a woman's clothes as she shed them at the cliff edge. So he climbed to the cliff-top meadows, and spread a net over short grass, and scattered grain, and ate the birds whose feet were entangled. He pushed thorn twigs into the earth around grain, and rock doves stuck their heads into the circle and were caught. He smeared twigs with the sticky sap of the fig tree, and caught the tiny rice bird, which he cleaned by pushing a straw down its throat and blowing.

He ate the birds at once, or only broke their wings so they were still fresh when he sold them in the town. He killed falcons and sold them as scarecrows to the riverside rice farmers, who hung them by the feet so that their wings spread. He trapped a crane and sewed its eyes shut, tethering it on the riverbank where it called down other cranes, which he killed. And he hatched duck eggs by the fire in the house, a blue thread hung above the eggs so that the ducklings followed the thread, tied to a cane, when he led them to eat snails in the rice fields by the river, then to the town to be killed, where he suffered much chaffing about lonely duckmen and their ducks.

May's birds didn't die. She caught eagles with a rabbit in a tethered basket: the eagle seized the rabbit but couldn't draw it through the basket and wouldn't let go, though May was coming with her net. She fed the eagle with meat tied to string, pulling the meat from its stomach until its spirit broke, and sold it to traders in the town. She took goshawks from the nest and trained them to hunt pheasants, then sold them to hunters; after two years they were released to breed. She found magpie nests, which are made with nothing from the ground, and sold them to a healer who burnt the nests to bake the eggs, which cured ailments caused by the earth element. And her pigeons flew to fields on the riverbank and returned at night to a coop above the house, their crops full of rice. She gave them water laced with alum so that they retched up the grain.

These pigeons were hard to train, but one hot night her brother killed them all, each fluttering wounded thing so funny that he killed another, a fist on his mouth to stop the laughter. Then he left, because he and May looked the same and there was a war about whether they'd be female or male.

'Stop,' said Tom. He sat up in the back of the van. 'Enough.'

He slid out of the doss bag and climbed into the passenger seat. It was dark and felt late. Bad dreams, bad thoughts, a sickness in the stomach. He opened the door and sat sideways with his feet on the road, sucking the cold. 'Enough of this pervy shit.'

Ten p.m.: he'd been asleep all day. He stamped along the street, the cold waking him up. He was near London Bridge Station when he stopped. He couldn't believe it: a Chinese takeaway called The Dream House.

He stared at the name. He walked away and caught his breath and came back. He put his face to the glass and had another revelation: all takeaways are the same – a square room converted from a house, and a counter near the back wall, though here the top was the wrong colour.

There was a Honda inside. With an effort he remembered the Tans' bike, and how he'd taken it to Bert the Breaker's. So this definitely wasn't the same one. It was older, now that he looked, and the food box was plastic not wood. But obviously it should be with a dog in a shed at the back.

He went inside. A Chinese calendar, Chinese posters, a TV on a stalk on the wall. No one behind the counter.

He lifted the flap and went through. For a second it was weird, but then he felt welcome and known.

The door to the kitchen had a frosted window and a clear plastic fingerplate. He pushed through and stopped. That old smell: steamed rice and sauce and chopped veg and the farty stink of cabbage. Men in aprons looked up but he ignored them. A new stove, and the dishwasher was nearer the door, but nothing too strange. The men were different, of course, but this was also good. A fresh start.

He lifted Chinese newspapers off a chair and sat down, hands on his knees, staring at everything. The men glanced at each other, but Tom looked with pleasure at the red tiles on the floor, the new white wall tiles.

He was so absorbed that the boy surprised him, saying 'Can I help you?' Tall, in a handsome sweater and ironed jeans.

Tom laughed. 'I know. You're a BBC: a British-Born Chinese. I mean, you're not an FOB: a Fresh Off the Boat. You're a banana: yellow on the outside, but white—'

'We're just closing, so . . .'

Now there was a girl. Big cheeks and glasses.

Tom looked at her with delight. Were they brother

51

and sister? He thought, 'When Chinese girls are plain they look like frogs— God, did I say that out loud?'

In a panic he held a hand up and said, 'Sorry. Sorry. I mean it's like white people. I mean they look a bit piggy sometimes, don't you think?'

The boy said, 'We're closing now.'

Concentrating, he said, 'I came in – in here – for a job. A job.'

The boy nodded. 'Right. But actually we're OK at the moment.'

Tom was stunned. After a moment he stood up. Head bowed, he moved towards the door.

The girl said, 'Maybe in the future.'

'No, no,' said the boy. 'Really.'

'I used to do deliveries. In a takeaway. But then there was this thing with marijuana, so I've not been well. But this place is so nice. It's like the old one. Like a mirror image or something: the same but not the same. And the name is great. It's perfect. And you as well, all of you, the same but new, so I thought . . .' Christ, I'm nearly crying.

'It's a Chinese restaurant,' said the boy. 'Normally we take Chinese people.'

They were at the street door. Tom murmured, 'I love Chinese people. Anything Chinese.'

He stepped onto the wet pavement. It was like when big Chung and little Wei had edged him onto the Whitechapel Road. He said, 'I was wondering: if there was a Chinese girl – I mean a girl who was just a baby in China, and then she came here, like you maybe, and she's never

believed in traditional stuff, Chinese beliefs and so on –
and then she splits up with her boyfriend, could she send
him dreams or visions or something? I mean send them to
her ex-boyfriend, when he's asleep.'

'I couldn't say.'

'The dreams might be bad, you know, because she's
still angry. So she'd send him bad dreams. Or she'd take
over his own dreams, and make them bad. What do you
think?'

'I don't know. Really.'

'Because if she did, then maybe it meant she still liked
him.'

Tom in the black street, his shoes wet, and rain glittering under the street lights. He looked into the takeaway.
'You're really lucky,' he said.

He touched the inside of the windscreen, where the mist
was gritty with forming ice. He rubbed his face, then
looked at his hands. Road dirt and engine oil deep in the
skin. 'It's from tinkering with the Honda.'

Why don't I ever mess with the van? It's too wrecked
and scary, that's why. He sat back, refusing to think
about anything except how he'd love to be a real mechanic: 'I get too angry.'

He squirmed into the seat, hands in his armpits. His
hands were black. Oil and coal dust. He worked on a
riverboat in China.

Tom put his head on the door pillar. Comfortable,
actually.

Steam, steel and the smell of coal. This was his life, and he didn't have to think about his dad or Johnny or anything.

Instead he sweltered below decks. Or else he'd take the air, staring up from a hatch at the laughing China girls who leaned on the rails, round bottoms in their black trousers, staring at the river until they turned and saw him with a shock, hands to their mouths at the red-faced devil popped up from below, who looked away quickly, his hand on the deck to feel the thumping engine, staring sideways at the girls because he'd travelled to China for women in trousers.

He came from London. There'd been a scandal over lady cyclists, and he'd stopped in the Whitechapel Road to watch a woman wobble past, her trousers and the pert saddle like a hand. These visions were rare so he'd travelled north, watching from a cobbled corner as women left the mine in canvas trousers. In an alley near the station he bought photographs, and the pictures mixed in his mind with the smell of coal and oil. Then he was breathless in a library, his eyebrows up, blushing over picture books of the rice women of Italy, who bent in flooded fields, trousers under their tucked-up skirts, until he thought of millions in the East, their trousers of cotton and silk that clung in the sultry air. So he sailed down the Thames, past Tower Bridge and Gravesend, and came to China and stared across the Canton docks, rapt with desire at the trousered multitudes, and nothing else would do.

He worked on the riverboats. The city women wore a skirt over their trousers, but upriver the women were poor and had no skirts, their trousers faded and shrunk tight, their lack his vertigo. So he came to an inland town. There was a pretty girl. Her strong hill-girl's legs. He followed her through steepening streets and she came to the foot of a great cliff, where a stream rioted down a cleft behind the town. Fearlessly she climbed, the black trousers tightening and loosening, up and up to a little house on the sheer cliff, where womanly garments dried on a tree.

The house was half on a ledge and half on beams driven into the black cliff. Around it were the lovely plants of the heights – mauve primulas, white and yellow roses – and people called it a 'sky-farm'.

In the van Tom thought, 'Oh, God.' But then he saw that May was lonely, so he didn't stop the dream. He saw how she would come to the town, sulky among the crowds, hoping that her brother had returned, but then she must climb again to the house, alone and angry. She dreamt of someone on the cliff, solemn with love in a field like a bed. Or she sat astride a peg and kicked her heels on the sheer cliff, daring a lover to climb from the town, but proud that she sat on pegs too thin for men.

Now she watched the foreigner near the house. She bent to her crops, thinking that he would stare. When she climbed back down the stranger had left, and her trousers were gone from the tree.

Down in the town the white man saw a beautiful girl. He said, 'It's the girl from the cliff.' But he was wrong: it was her brother.

'Shit,' thought Tom.

May's brother had travelled far. After he left home he had wandered with the bee-keepers, who carry their hives upriver in spring, following the flowers, then to the lowlands in autumn for the blooming of the winter plum. A girl wanted him, but she made him think of falling from a cliff, so he turned to the river, sleeping in summer in a fold of the riverbank, and in winter in a fishing town, curled among sacks in an alley or on nets on the shingle. He made a musket with a pipe stolen from a round-eye riverboat, and mixed sulphur, charcoal, and bird lime into bad powder which burnt with a hiss, scattering chopped wire at the river birds. One winter he lived off bats, stretching a net over a cave mouth and coming at dusk and dawn to take their breast meat, purple and gamey, throwing the shrieking bats into the river, although he didn't hate them like the birds. He smoked out the last bats with fires of damp straw, and they were easy targets as they circled the cave roof. He tied driftwood into a kind of bonnet, and floated among wild ducks on the river, pulling them suddenly under by the feet so that the flock didn't scare. He sold the ducks to the riverboat crews and drank his profits because he didn't know if he desired his twin or desired to resemble her. One night, very drunk, he lifted a tavern door from its hinges and launched it onto the river, carried downstream for a week until he reached the great road to the capital. Just outside the Forbidden City was the shack of the knifers.

He paid six taels and lay on the low couch, held by three men, his parts numbed with chilli sauce and removed with a single pass of the curved knife, the wound dressed with wet paper. For three days he burned with thirst and a desire to piss. The brass plug was removed and his urine flowed, which meant he would live.

He entered the Forbidden City and his looks brought him a place with the Imperial players. But he was ignorant and ill-tempered and played silent roles as a serving maid or concubine. He thought, 'My sister is pretty and we are twins, so I'm too pretty for this.' He was whipped for idleness and fled to a nearby town, but was followed in the street by cries of 'crow' because of his high voice and 'stinking eunuch' because of his wayward bladder. So the Eunuch Police found him and took him back to the Forbidden City and gave him twenty strokes of the bamboo.

He was still proud and lazy and received a hundred strokes. He had three days to recover, then received a whipping called 'lifting the scabs'. He ran away again, for which the penalty was death.

He had stolen a box of gold and could buy medicines to supply the yang – the male essence. He didn't want his parts to regrow, but he hoped that his voice might deepen and his body lose its roundness so he might escape the Eunuch Police.

The medicines didn't work and he stayed indoors, obliged to trust his servant – a grinning villain who chewed garlic and stole his food.

Sperm is pure yang, so he sent the servant to bribe a prostitute. There was no effect and he thought, 'Perhaps the fluid must be fresh, and without female liquids.' He sent the servant to buy parts from the executioner. Again he was disappointed, and thought, 'Perhaps all potency is lost at the moment of death, even though the parts are warm.'

So he clubbed his servant with a log from the fire, and used his precious parts, then killed him. There was no effect and he despaired.

He returned upriver, wanting to visit his home town before he was killed. Here he saw a Westerner, smeared with coal dust, smelling of oil. He shuddered at the hairy hands and lumpy face, but surely they showed an excess of yang, so he stole May's clothes.

He smiled, and the white demon bought him tea. He was coy, and the monster sweated. With a show of reluctance he went to the barbarian's room. To please the white ghost he sat with his ankle on his knee, or with a foot on the table, or he leaned on a window sill like a woman at a ship's rail. After three days a black hair sprouted on his arm.

But then the changes stopped. He thought, 'Perhaps the foreigner is bored, as men grow bored, no longer giving the thick fluid which comes from the spine and makes sons.' He pleased the Westerner in strange ways and the barbarian was enslaved, so he climbed to his old home on the cliff. May greeted him with joy, but he seized her throat.

'I'm leaving with the white monster,' he said. 'But first I'll kill you and dress you as me and throw you from the cliff, so the Eunuch Police will think I'm dead. And I'll take your clothes and be you and everyone will say, "How pretty she is."'

But May twisted free and ran from the house and across the little garden and down the bamboo ropes. Her brother was close behind, and caught her on a narrow ledge above the town. Here they fought until a slim figure fell to the water and floated downstream and was found a week later and claimed by the Eunuch Police.

By this time, though, the white man and his lover were far away. They sailed downstream to Canton and lived in the Western quarter, a scandal to Chinese and Westerners alike. But the white man was proud of his lovely companion, and spent his wages on trousers of canvas and cotton and silk.

9

Tom woke up fighting. Someone was crushing his face. For a while he roared and kicked, his head cruelly held. Then he stopped because he was alone.

He'd tumbled into the footwell of the van. He was blind and suffocated, stuck between the seat and the gear stick, his feet tangled in the pedals. He lay for a while, smelling old mud on the carpet, his neck crooked, remembering how the dream had made him twist and groan.

Six a.m. Cold and still dark. He hauled himself free, his back sore, and started driving while he was half asleep. On the Whitechapel Road he parked across from the hospital, desperate to see May but instead watching a woman shivering on a street corner. A Whitechapel trollop, just like the Ripper killed. And probably the local Chinkies were suspects, pitiless insect faces, they chop suey then they chop us.

He frowned because the dreams weren't just about May and bad dads and an outsider who might be him: there was also this stuff about pervy brothers.

He jumped out and rubbed the windows with his sleeve. Christ, get me out of London. He nodded because it was obvious. Bastard place. But drive for long enough and it ends, just like anywhere else.

Back shivering in the van, thinking about the black

beyond the last lights, and how he'd wake up shivering but at least it's the country. He could get a job. He'd be brown and fit. Hedging and ditching, then evenings in the pub with a dog on his feet. Shit, he could steal the Tans' dog. Poor bugger, it would love to run. He saw it muddy and laughing, still mad and crapping everywhere but getting better, galloping round the garden where he's digging veg for May. He straightens, stretching his stiff back, then rinses muddy carrots in a bucket by the door, grabbing herbs from a window box, and into their little thatched house, the roof over its eyes like a slipped wig, where they're happy and alone.

He'd talk to her. Somehow get her out of London. And steal the dog.

He was falling asleep when the Aussie doc walked past.

Tom watched him, amazed. He crawled from the van, stiff with cold, and stared after the bouncy gangling figure under the street lights. 'Well, I suppose the dick has to go home sometime.' He got the washing line off the back doors, cold clumsy hands, and ran after him. He remembered an alley up ahead and made a noose in the line, laughing as he ran. Cleaners and labourers at the bus stops and a few cars going past in the dark. Easy to pick the moment.

He dropped the noose over the doctor's head. He turned and put the line over his shoulder and hauled Frank up the alley, enjoying the gurgles and gasps, the Aussie bastard dragging on his back, holding the noose, kicking himself along. Tom hooked the line through railings, and pulled until Frank hit them with a thump.

He looped the line around the bugger's ankles, the doc trying to kick but too busy pawing at his neck. Laughing, skipping around, Tom dropped the line around a spike at the top of the railings and hauled him upside down. Now Frank was gripping the rails, so it was easy to fasten his bony brown wrists. The doc's tie flopped down over his face: Tom pushed it into his mouth for a gag.

He strolled back to the van, rubbing his hands. He meant to leave the bugger for a while in the cold, but he sat fidgeting in the van and then ran back.

He crept into the alley. Dark in here, though the sky was brightening. He laughed. Long Frank was still upside down on the railings, pop-eyed and grunting through the gag, and no one had come. Tom admired the loops of line around the wrists and ankles and across the mouth to hold in the tie, then he crouched to whisper.

'I might let you go, pal. I might let you go. But first you have to tell me something.' He loosened the line across the doc's mouth and waited till he spat out the tie. 'Right. Any shouting and your teeth are on the deck.'

'You . . .'

'Yes? Want to say something? Maybe you'd better say nothing. Better just answer the question. Here it is. You ready?'

'I . . .'

'Shut up. OK. Think carefully. Here's what I want to know: how did Johnny die?'

The doctor frowned, bewildered.

'Not hard, Frankie baby. You must know. Come on: how?'

'But it's not a secret, for God's sake.'

'Just answer, OK.'

'It was in the bloody paper.'

'OK. Fine. Just answer the question, all right?'

'Stabbed himself with scissors. In the groin. Bled to death.'

'Right. All right. Not hard, was it.'

'Let me down.'

'Certainly. No problem.'

He undid the line, cutting it to leave one wrist tied to the railings with many knots, trying to think of a smart comment.

The doc said, 'It was in the damn paper.'

'Good,' said Tom. 'I'm glad.'

'What does *that* mean?'

Tom hurried back to the van and drove, the back doors flapping. He got out and water was running over his feet. Some sort of flood or burst main. He tied the doors with washing line and got into the driver's seat. Damn shoes have been wet for months, big-toe nails poking through the cloth.

He sat for a long time, thinking about Johnny with the scissors. 'Of course.'

When the daylight was too horrible he started the van. He parked outside Brixton Tube, women climbing out to the pavement. But it was hopeless, sitting in a stink of ill-luck. May's fault.

He saw two Chinese boys across the road, big Chinese-Brits with thick smooth chip-fed limbs. He jumped out and stood up and shouted gleefully, 'Hey, Chinky boys. Fly lice? Wery wery dericious. Fly lice, OK?'

The boys stared, then Tom remembered Johnny and drove off disgusted. He parked in a side street, listening as the engine cooled and ticked.

'I should call Dad.' So he pictured the phone in their crappy front room, and this was a distraction. On weekdays it sat on the little altar between a gilt cup and two plastic incense holders. And his dad would say, 'Hello. This is Convocator Lawson,' because he ran the Gathering of the Brotherhood of the Golden Dawn, a wilfully retro cult founded by Tom's granddad, a wiry working man who sat behind his moustache in a fading picture on the mantelpiece, knees apart in his Sunday suit, flat cap folded in his big foundryman's hands, and what seemed like a frown of special enquiry for Tom. And every Friday, which he called 'the Sabbath', Tom's dad stood among his devotees, dangerously near the gas fire in their little front room on the scruffy council estate, his linen robes wafting, the shiny black toecaps poking out.

He loved his leather shoes, black for Friday and brown for the week. Straight-backed, he strode through the dingy streets with a crunch of gravel – he didn't drive and was proud of it. And there were shoe-stands and shoe-stretchers and a proper wooden bootbox with brushes and rags and tins for the weekly clean, into which Tom was sometimes inducted till he maddened his father again, particularly in the matter of insteps, which must also be polished. Then little Gillian got old enough, and was a natural polisher.

Soon after, his dad did something awful and his mum walked out so that she wouldn't have to talk about it. Lawson was satisfied: he'd always said she was pointless, weeping on the sofa or creeping about with a damp hanky, pretty and silly, only useful for making their problems seem trivial. Now she'd gone like a scapegoat. He said, 'You weren't breastfed. Not a drop. Bad for her figure or something,' so Tom cried less.

His dad also triumphed over the neighbours. He got punched at the factory and went on the dole, his windows were smashed and Tom's friends stopped calling. But his church didn't suffer, being based on the cunning idea that the dead would speak through the bereaved. In the poky front room, widows reminisced or aired old rows, till Lawson said, 'Let him talk,' and sometimes the woman felt her dead husband speak through her lips, giving his side of things but saying that perhaps she'd been right after all. His dad – rouged and handsome – would raise a hand, a blessing and a barrier, and draw himself up, straight-backed on his leather heels like wood that made Tom fear for his toes.

Tom was the altar boy. In a green nylon jacket he'd greet the whiskered women, who bent to kiss him. But then they'd change. Tom held the wine and wafers on a plastic tray, but if the women moaned for their dead he'd tremble and his dad would rescue the tray. He wrung his hands if the widows did, and if they wailed then his eyeballs bulged till he thought they'd pop out.

He took a hammer from a shop and cycled past parked cars, whose wing mirrors he smashed. Crossed by his dad or a teacher he ran to butt them, or put his head down and swung his fists crabwise, the men trying to guard their bollocks with dignity.

Because of his dad, life at school was a solitude interrupted by fights. But still he talked about adventures with his classmates, his dad impatient then angry: 'So we climbed on the roof only there was this big bird, like a crow, probably a crow, and it tried to peck us and it did peck us, not me but the others, only we killed it, I killed it, and then the teacher came and we came down, and then,' his dad walking away and Tom breathless but unstoppable, trotting behind, waving his hands, his elbows pinned to his sides.

Then he grew spotty and his dad was disgusted. Tom had to wash his own underpants, and his dad still cooked for him but couldn't watch him eat, and wore washing-up gloves to collect his plate. Gillian was tolerated, although illness was making her messy.

And there were new women at the services, younger and louder, not widows, often not wives, who came for a week or two and then got bored, talking about men who drank or fought or stole, the ones who left and the new ones who came. The widows didn't approve, shaking their wattled throats, lipstick on crooked, but his dad had a new giggle, virginal and shrill.

He told Tom, 'You always creep about. Why? When I walk about, people hear me coming,' and he stamped his leather heels, Tom thinking, 'That's just about it.' Later he understood: his dad was going deaf. But Tom was sixteen and unforgiving. He'd left school, and had lost his place at the séances to pretty twin brothers, recruited as they waited for their mum in a supermarket car park. So he idled through that summer with plastic soldiers from his childhood, who sniped across the sofa or fell to the carpet with drawn-out cries, until his dad said, 'This is Mrs Walston.'

She was a health visitor who affected to be harassed. She'd come to see Gilly but stayed for the service, sitting forward on her chair, glancing at the window and the door and back to Lawson, as if ready to listen although her days were full, her hair pulled back to a clip like a bear trap. Afterwards she shook Tom's hand with her arm straight. 'You can help Harold,' she said.

And this, now that he thought about it, was where the whole China thing began.

10

Tom dreamt that May was dreaming. She was on a bunk in the nurses' room but thought she was going up the stairs at the takeaway.

The wallpaper was ripped. She pulled the rip and found a door and another set of stairs. She went up the stairs to a dusty room. The room was beautiful, with a balcony over the river and stairs down to another door. She went down and pulled the door and heard a ripping noise and peered through torn paper to a nice flat.

She crept away and cleaned the room and one day Tom came from the other flat. They were happy in the room but her father spoiled it all.

'No,' said Tom, stirring in the van.

He put himself on a tractor. May was planting rice. She heard the tractor and straightened, barefoot in the muddy water. She smiled, shading her eyes with her brown hand.

'China,' he thought. 'China.'

Tom dreamt that May dreamt that she was free. She was out of London, happy in the country. She had leather wristbands and boots made of fur. She had a short skirt. A short leather skirt.

She was a bandit and led a gang of bandits. They were all women. They wore leather skirts and ran bare-breasted through the mountains. They bathed in the river, splashing and bold, and then danced naked in secret groves, and men sometimes hid to watch, though if they were caught they died.

The women danced to praise the goddess. This wasn't the fertility goddess of men, who pray for sons or a rich harvest or fat fish. Instead it was the goddess of a woman's self-love as she looks down at her body, her emblems being the moon over water, a marsh flower, the prow of a boat.

The women got dressed. They painted their faces, each painting another. They hid by the river road. When travellers came they spared the women but told the men, 'We'll cut off your head or your precious parts. Choose.' And the men who gave up their parts were dressed as women and did the lowest work while the bandits pleasured each other.

But May had a secret: as the moon changed so did her body. Every month she said, 'I'm going to the mountains, to talk to the goddess.' But actually the moon was growing and so were her precious parts.

So May crossed the mountains and for two weeks she was a man and the chief of a gang of men. When travellers came May said, 'Stab the child so the parents are helpless.' The bandits spared young men but killed the women and children and staked the husbands to the ground, May cross-legged on their chests, watching their eyes dim, saying, 'You told your wives to run with the children, but they stood shrieking, their hands to their mouths, or they shrieked and held your arm. And so you die.'

In each gang there was a lieutenant who was the chief's lover. One month, when May left the gang of women, her lieutenant secretly followed her into the mountains. At the same time May's male lieutenant came to the mountains, wanting to know where his chief spent half the month.

The lieutenants watched from their hiding places as May crossed the river waist-deep and emerged as a man. Their spears met in his heart.

But then they wept. They saw each other weeping and embraced. They lived together in the mountains, talking often of their beloved chief who was dead, and at first they were chaste but later they were husband and wife, until the two gangs killed them and fought a battle where many died.

'No,' said Tom, awake in the van.

He put himself with May in Chinatown. They were in a caff, sitting stiffly. He said, 'It'd be great, you know, if we could get back together.'

They stared out the window. May said, 'What about a job?'

'Yes. Definitely.'

'Not the takeaway.'

'No, no.'

'Is that a beard?'

'I'll shave.'

'You smell.'

'Yes. Sorry. A bath, straight away.'

Even her dad was fine. On Sunday afternoons he took Tom to Chinatown, Mr Tan fat but sprightly, dapper in a flat cap, his white shirt open sportingly at the throat, playing poker with his pals in a Gerrard Street basement, salty snacks in a glass dish, his fat fingers spread on the cards, Tom staring at their lips and eyes but now he was learning Cantonese. 'More Chinese than damn Chinese boys,' said Mr Tan. He put the fag in his mouth to shake with the other managers, and then they were off to the wholesalers, Tom heaving fat bags of rice into the car boot, trays of floppy-headed greens on the back seat, and back to Whitechapel, Tan angry at his English son-in-law, but what can you do.

Asleep, Tom said, 'I'll be the son you lost.'

Tom dreamt that May dreamt that she was a bandit's daughter. She lived by a fast river, very arrogant towards her father's men and towards a poor boy who roamed along the river, fishing and begging for rice water and killing birds with a sling.

One day in a rage she locked her door. The bandit said, 'Whoever opens her door is my friend.' But the girl ignored the threats and persuasions of the bandit and his men.

That night the boy went to her door. He crouched down and miaowed like a kitten until she silently drew the bolt. The bandit rushed in while she cursed the boy.

The bandit was pleased with the boy, but his lieutenant said, 'Beware, because he is called "Cunning Orphan".

When he was young his family were crossing the forest. The boy complained so they left him and a witch came and put him on her back and ran towards her den. The boy pushed his fingers in her eyes, but she laughed and said, "I'm blind, little one," and ran even faster through the trees. The boy said, "I'm small. But my father is fat, and my mother is pretty, and my sister is young and sweet." So the boy led the witch after his family. First she caught the little girl. Then the mother, who wasn't pretty but the witch couldn't see. Then the father, who reached their house but she broke the door and killed him. Now the witch was full of blood and the boy said, "Tie me to this tree, aunt, so you can sleep." The witch tied him with rope and fell asleep. But the tree was only the broken doorpost and the boy climbed up the post and lifted the rope off the post and killed the witch and that's how he was named.'

The bandit grew thoughtful. He sent for the boy and said, 'Read my dream. I dream every night that I'm beheaded and my head lies in a grey field.'

The boy lied to the bandit. 'Your dream was nothing,' he said. 'Swim in the river.'

The bandit swam in the river and the boy said, 'See? Your head is like a severed head in a grey field.' The bandit's men praised the boy, though May spat and said, 'He's a stupid beggar.'

Now the bandit's men came to the boy with their dreams. He always found a happy answer, so the men paid him and said, 'He should marry our chief's daughter.'

May heard this talk and said, 'Never!' and took a

secret lover among the men. But her father suspected and called his men together and said that the boy would search out who had spoiled his daughter.

May cried, 'He'll trick you. Above all, don't be afraid.'

But the boy told them, 'I've seen your dreams and now I'll see your hearts. In the evening I'll call you together and smell your loins and smell out who enjoyed this girl.'

That night the bandit's men were called together and the boy went sniffing among them. Of course he smelled nothing, but then he smelled a man who had perfumed his loins. It was the bandit's lieutenant, who was beheaded while May shrieked her hate.

May devised a trick. The bandit had a jewelled knife which was the symbol of his rule, but now it vanished. May said, 'That beggar boy, your great wizard, can see six feet into the earth. But can he find the knife?'

The boy saw that this was his biggest test. On the first day he burned spices and odorous woods, and May came jeering and said, 'Have you found the knife?'

He said, 'I see it vaguely,' so that May ceased to smile.

Next day the boy danced and sang and May came again and said, 'Have you found the knife?'

He said, 'I see it more clearly,' and May went away angry.

On the third day he fasted and prayed, sitting cross-legged and calling on the Enlightened One. May came again, but before she could speak the boy looked into her eyes and said, 'Now I see the knife.'

In her anger and fear May threw the jewelled knife in the dust and said, 'Keep my secret or I'll kill you.'

The boy took the knife to the bandit, saying that he'd found it in the dust, and he was rewarded and said, 'Now I'll marry your daughter.'

The bandit said, 'But she hates you.'

'I've seen into her eyes and overmastered her.'

'But you are a beggar boy!' said the bandit.

So the boy took the jewelled knife and cut off the bandit's head, which rolled in the grey dust, and the bandit's men took him as their leader, and he told May to marry him.

Instead she killed herself. She sat cross-legged in the Underworld, sitting on bones and chewing bones and pleasuring herself with a leg bone, the hair down over her face.

11

Tom in a pub toilet, washing his wounds: a cut eye, sore ribs, blood in his nose. He'd been stumbling through Brixton, forced from the van by the dreams, which had followed him through the evening streets while he blundered across the market, bumping people till the dream worked itself out, May pleasuring herself in hell as he reeled under the viaduct. Then he'd seen the same two big Chinese-British boys.

He couldn't fight. He'd watched them come, and put up his hands at the last minute, bowing humbly after the first punch, going down with a roaring in his ears. Then it was a rough pub all night, sipping a half in a corner, blood in his nose, until it was time for the van.

He walked to the side street, head down but watching for watchers. Not the back doors, too obvious, so he got in the driver's side then over the seats and onto the mattress. He pissed out of a rust hole in the wheel arch, the piss dropping smooth and straight from his new dick, where it had once spattered childishly in barley-sugar spirals. He was aching for a smoke, but it was damned cold so he slid into the doss bag, the dusty rug pulled over him, his eye and ribs and stitches sore.

'I need a girl.' A girl and a room. He'd be happy, and the dreams would stop. But he shivered, thinking about

Western girls: 'I might not manage it.' Only a China girl would do. They all want white boys anyway. You see them with a Chinese boyfriend. Useless, like a sister. A bit of sweat and stubble: that's what's needed. Not a black man: that's too much. Just a little whiff of the sweaty bollocks. 'If I can just lose my cherry.'

He shivered and got warm. The pleasure of hiding. Peace after his beating, but God knows he didn't want to sleep, so he lay in the doss bag and thought about the pool hall and big Chung saying, 'You friend from hospital.'

Actually it was a nursing home. On his first morning Tom took two buses to the next town, where Mrs Walston brought him tea on the kitchen steps until Harold appeared – a huge old man with the look of a stunned ox, complete with a dent in his forehead which the sledge-hammer could have made. And he was being steered from behind: stepping out from his wake was a stocky boy a little older than Tom. In a flat Scottish accent he said, 'Enjoy the little man,' and then left.

Harold led him around the overgrown lawns and weedy flowerbeds, his big boots turned out at the toes, gesturing vaguely, a rumble in his chest betokening the good advice he couldn't now deliver. Suddenly he lumbered off down a brick path, Tom following through dripping rhododendrons, under a trellis dragged down by a rampant climbing rose, and on to the shed. Harold edged his great sofa shoulders through the door, squeezed past a mower, nodding and rumbling with good advice he thought he was giving, and sat with a bump on a sack of fertilizer. He blinked with surprise, opened a greaseproof package on his lap, his huge thighs coyly together, and slowly ate a cheese-and-jam sandwich, his eyes bewildered over bulging cheeks as if at uncalled-for dentistry.

Tom stroked the mower. It was a big red tricycle, very old, with handlebars and levers and a rusty engine on the front wheel. A scrap of floral carpet padded its steel seat. Its smells filled the shed. Harold sucked his dentures, occasionally passing a hand over his eyes like wiping away cobwebs, so Tom climbed onto the mower, working the levers, until at last the old man took bigger and bigger sighs, as if pumping himself up to speak.

'Edge the lawn,' he said in a rush. 'New gardener. Edge the lawn.' Then he fell asleep.

Next day Tom was alone. He sat for a while in the shed, but even the mower couldn't hold him. Towards lunchtime he took a spade and began trimming around the huge front lawn. Once he looked up and nearly dropped the spade: ten feet away, Harold sat behind the murky glass of the old folks' lounge, his great hands empty, watching him open-mouthed. In the afternoon Mrs Walston bustled out in her sensible shoes, a pencil in her tight hair, and said, 'Goodness. What a difference already.'

Next day it rained. By ten o'clock he'd eaten his sandwiches, cleaned the spade, cut his finger on a bill-hook, oiled the shears, and stared over the dripping garden. Mostly, though, he sat on the mower. From this perch he noticed a high shelf. He was searching along the shelf among starved spiders, boxes of ten-year-old seeds, woodworm dust, shrivelled seed potatoes, when he found the manual. He looked at its oily thumbprints, its talk of hundredweights and quarts, and saw that the mower was as old as his dad.

Then he found Harold's name. It was written square and clear on the flyleaf, and in the margins were numbers and diagrams and notes. Tom pictured him in his active days, and himself as Harold's apprentice and then his son, the old man saying, 'In the two-stroke engine, oil is mixed with the petrol to serve as the engine lubricant,' and when they went to the tool shop they went to the trade counter and the salesman winked and said, 'Here comes trouble.'

Tom read the manual all that day, stayed an hour after knocking-off time because he couldn't understand carburettors, and took it home to read at the kitchen table and then in bed, sawdust and oily cobwebs on the sheets, working his arm to understand pistons, his eyebrows near the hairline at these parts that were hidden but followed rules.

He fell asleep and thought he was Harold. He was on the mower in his boiler suit and flat cap, his steel-toed boots turned out, then tramping back to the shed, lifting his knapsack off a hook behind the door, his old army number on the flap, and inside was milk in a pill bottle, sugar and tea leaves in a twist of silver paper, and a cheese-and-jam sandwich, which was delicious. So in the morning Tom was ready for the mower.

On the way to work he bought petrol and oil with his own money. The engine was rusty so he doubled the dose of oil. Later that afternoon everyone in the nursing home looked up, because the mower had no silencer. Then the windows went dark as blue smoke drifted across.

Tom blamed this notoriety on the old folk in the garden. First a trembling man stood by the boundary wall, blind and smiling, facing into a weedy corner. Then a woman was parked by the compost heap, her wheelchair tracks through Tom's freshly planted peas. She couldn't raise her head, but gave him a throaty knowing chuckle. Finally Harold returned to the shed. He was sat in his old corner, his feet in a sack of tulip bulbs, his cap on upside down, staring at the wall with noble indignation: 'The Scotch one,' he said. 'The Scotch one and the other one.'

Tom led him to the house. The Scottish boy was sitting on the wooden ramp to the side door, watching him through cigarette smoke. Next to him stood a boy with greasy blond hair, who put his fag in his mouth and clapped slowly. Tom stared with his eyebrows up and the blond laughed. 'We've been watching you,' he said.

He was called Charlie. 'We don't do any work,' he said at once. 'And they can't send us home because our dads are Friends of the Trustees.' He glanced admiringly at his friend. 'He's got a gang. They do shoplifting and they burn things. Barns and things, in Ayrshire. And they, like, stampede cows into rivers, don't you, Mac. I think that's really funny.'

Mac said, 'We've got a proposition.'

Every night Tom met them on his way to the bus stop. They had a rota of local towns where they stole from cars at petrol pumps, and Tom was a new face to get cashback on the debit cards. Afterwards they celebrated in cafes – Mac the restrained commander, Charlie laughing coffee down his nose because the people walking past were all ugly, like they were half chicken or half lizard or something, and Tom weak with relief, hunched over, his eyebrows up, watching their lips and eyes because they were eighteen and quietly posh, so that Mac said in his drab voice, 'He should come to our dormitory, should young Tom.'

Charlie looked eagerly at Mac, giggling until he got a punch in the ribs. 'Try punching me, you shit,' thought Tom. He wasn't going anywhere near their room, but he'd also no desire to go home early, his dad angry, the TV too loud, and Gillian dizzy and scared. He said, 'You know, sometimes the ignition keys are still in.'

That's how they found the Pub of Slags. Whenever they stole a car, Tom drove to the cheap housing estate and the one-storey pub with its flat roof, leaving them with the fat wives and going out through parked prams to tinker cluelessly in the car park through the long summer evenings, fingers shaky with nerves then irritation, maybe taking a wheel off or gapping the plugs so that it spluttered all the way back, the engine following rules that he didn't know. If they went with the women (the uglier the funnier), he delved deeper, once taking the cylinder head off a souped-up BMW for joy of its lovely tools, but the cambelt fell inside and they had to walk back to town – Mac furious on his sinister short thick legs that made his arse wag, Charlie dancing round him like a dog, and Tom baffled and lagging behind because he could never believe that a plan had failed: he would stare at a bolt-head he'd rounded or a finger he'd cut, but only saw what should have happened. If he went back to the pub, surely the Beemer would be fine.

One afternoon Johnny Tan walked past the cafe. He saw them, hesitated, gave a twisted grin, and slid inside with the door minimally open, coming to their table almost sideways with shyness, his thin legs only breaking his pants at the knee, like a man on stilts.

'Our new dorm-mate,' said Mac, and Charlie said loudly, 'They don't do flied dog and shit,' though Johnny had a London voice, clever and quick.

But maybe he recognized another misfit, so he was with Tom in the pub car park when Bert the Breaker turned up. Tom was working on an Audi with his fancy BMW tools while Johnny tweaked the radio. He got Chinese T-shirts from a friend of his dad, choosing them by their slogans: this one said 'Travel! Living for easy and pleasant', and was somehow like his nervous rehearsed jokes that 'China is really advanced, you know, because they shave with lasers,' and 'He who laughs last laughs longest, as my father always says,' and 'Confucius say: Horse have four legs, but run more fast than centipede,' all of which made Charlie laugh, but in the wrong way.

For no reason, Tom was trying to get a front wheel off. But two of the bolts wouldn't shift, and he was sweating and desperate in the heat, his knees sticking to the soft tar, Johnny staring down from the driver's seat, his smooth arm on the door. Irritated, Tom said,

'I suppose you're getting on OK with those two. In the dormitory.'

'My. A very leading question.' Tom bent back to work.

Johnny said, 'Nothing so unappealing could be imagined.' He rapped his knuckles softly on the hot door. 'The real puzzle is why *you* waste your time with them. Mine too, actually. Shouldn't you grow out of it? You're not Charlie, after all.'

Then a skinny man in a baseball cap and tight oily jeans said, 'Put the jack under the end of the wrench, for fuck's sake,' and afterwards flashed a wad of twenties, so the gang had cash and Tom took car-theft lessons, doing the risky bits while Bert parked around the corner, engine running, angry because Tom always sat for a while in the cars, breathing other people's lives. 'You'll never be a natural,' said Bert, wiping his hands on his jeans, 'but you're mad enough.'

It was the end of summer. Johnny was going to medical school, having practised nursing at the home, and Charlie and Mac were off to university. But they'd shown Tom another way to live: he would go to London.

To celebrate he stole a Peugeot 205 GTi he'd been watching for weeks, and followed the bus route home, Mac and Charlie in the back shouting, 'Tom, we're lost,' and Johnny in the passenger seat, getting the breeze where Tom had pushed his fingers in the top of the door and bent it out till he could hook a wire onto the lock, Peugeots being made of tin.

He was nervous as he stood in front of the house, Mac staring around like a general, Johnny climbing tentatively out into the heat, and Charlie on the Pug roof shouting, 'Look at me,' dancing and stamping in pink sunglasses from the glove compartment.

'It's the Sabbath, of course,' said Tom's dad, at the front door in a surplice. 'You would bring guests on a Sabbath.' And Charlie laughed because here was the pure original of Tom's yokel burr.

'Say hello to Tom's little sis,' said Lawson, and they all looked at Gilly, sitting in the window, smiling and tearful at these boys she might have married. 'Her first wheelchair came today, but it's a big secret. And now someone has to fetch it from the shed, don't you, Tom.'

The wheelchair was old and clumsy, the handles sticky as he hauled it around the house, under the dripping toilet overflow, the rotten window frames, over the weeds in the concrete path, and parked by the front door: 'And?'

'Get Gillian.'

The front room was dim and cool. She sat in the pale light by the window. 'Hello, babe,' he whispered. He held his breath and dived down, pushing his hands underneath and carrying her outside, her old lady's smell, laying her in the chair, her numb hands curled.

His dad strode off, but the chair was stupid and heavy, the gang helping him through the gate, Gilly mewing in shame. Tom said, 'Thanks, all. Now bugger off, please,' and he hurried across the estate, the gardens full of car bits and staked dogs, his dad soaring ahead in his linen gown, a drunk shouting, 'You.'

There was a proper meeting hall – a wooden summer house that smelt of incense and candles and stood in the garden of a widow and one-time benefactor who'd worked with Lawson on the decorating and had driven him in the evenings to country pubs, her fat Jaguar jamming the lanes, till finally she understood. She started nagging him for rent, and had cut off the power, though the other ladies said what did it matter in this lovely summer. She watched from the lounge window, gripping the curtain as Lawson and his followers entered through a side gate of her long garden. There were only four in the congregation, dropping cash into a box held by a long-haired youth, who assessed Tom with a pout.

The service was a parody of the Church of England. His dad's drawl was worse, more insultingly negligent as it echoed off the whitewashed walls, his long head turned away, until abruptly he sat down and crossed his arms and scowled, the women standing doubtful, hand in hand, waiting for the spirits as Gillian whimpered into the silence.

Tom began to drift, feeling the old terrors. He tumbled out, lit a cigarette, and wandered the garden till he couldn't hear, sitting on a roller, forcing himself to look at the greased bracket that held the axle, and how the roller was in two halves so that it cornered better.

'He's getting worse, your dad,' said the pouting youth, a little too close, staring down, nervous and snooty like Johnny, tight trousers tucked into funny black pixie boots.

'Not really.'

'Well, you haven't seen him,' said the boy. 'Wait till he goes off on one.'

Tom, elbows on knees, stared through his smoke at the restless boots with their wrinkled pointy toes and sticking-up tabs at the back.

The boy said, 'I have to get out of this dump.'

'Good luck.'

'I bet you're not coming back. I bet you're going somewhere with a bit of life.'

Tom thought: 'My dad bought those boots.'

The boy said, 'I wondered. We could meet up.'

'Look, no offence, but fuck off.'

'Fair enough.' The boots turned away. 'But your old man is mad.'

After the service they waited while the ladies gushed at his dad, the summer breeze flapping his robes, white lace in the sunshine, and then Tom pushed Gilly home: her trembling old-woman's head, but bright girlish hairs at the nape. He said, 'How do you manage?'

'I never take her,' said Lawson, pleased at his trick. 'So it was kind of you to volunteer.' He followed as Tom carried her to the kitchen, then said, 'Where did you get the car?'

Tom shrugged, but it seemed after all to be a real question. 'It's borrowed. I mean it's from a friend.'

'Very kind, your friend.' He flung his gown in the washing machine. There were grey tufts on his cheekbones. 'So now I understand the Scotch accent. All of a sudden you're Scottish, because of that thug.' His twisted mouth; white cottony stuff in the corners. 'No, go to London. We'll be fine. Plenty of thick widows. And Gillian doesn't care. She can't say the days now, have

you noticed. Go on, ask her: Monday, Tuesday, Pilchards
. . . Whatnot. This kind friend, did he or she ask if you
were insured? Or is that too boring?'

'A bit boring, Dad.'

'But you parked in front of the house. With your mates
carrying on.'

'Don't shout.'

'And now they're doing God knows what, then coming
back here.'

'Jesus, not so loud. Why are you angry?'

'Because this is my home.' Gilly was flapping her arms.

'Christ. Well, they don't have to come back. Neither
do I, in fact.'

'Dadda,' said Gilly, starting to cry.

Tom drove to the High Street and sat on a wall by the
Thames, here only a track of green reeds along a hidden
ditch, watching until Mac and Charlie appeared, Johnny
trailing hopefully behind. On the drive back he couldn't
speak, gripping the steering wheel until his arms ached,
not thinking about Gilly's curled useless hands, which
she'd push in his pockets when she was little, giggling as
she stole his change. Johnny cleared his throat in the
silence and said, 'Tom's dad was / Cross-dressed with an
actual cross.'

'Not again,' said Charlie. 'Crap rap. The world's only
black Chinky.'

At midnight, in a suburb of Reading, Tom parked and
grabbed a bit of silver paper from the ashtray. 'Watch.'
He got out and smashed the side indicator of a Mazda

MX-5, then laid silver paper on the bulb holder. He bounced on the bonnet and the alarm chirruped and died, its fuse burned out. He broke a window and got in, working in the footwell with his tools in the smell of someone's life, grinding his teeth when he thought about Gilly.

Mac said, 'I'll have the Mazda,' and drove off, so Tom took Johnny and Charlie back a couple of miles in the Pug then crashed into a parked Mondeo. He drove around the block, by which time Charlie had finished swearing and the alarm had stopped. No one had come, but the airbags had fired, meaning that the doors were unlocked – helpful to paramedics and thieves. Charlie took the Ford, saying, 'You're the Napoleon of car crime.'

Tom had read something about Brixton squats, and he was dropping Johnny off along the way. But with all the arsing about it was too late. Anyway, the Pug had been spilling coolant since they'd hit the Mondeo, so they were cadging water at every garage, but when they got to London there were no garages and the engine seized near Tower Bridge. It was dawn when they got to an alley off the Whitechapel Road.

They crept through the kitchen and up the stairs to Johnny's room. Tom threw a pillow on the floor and lay down saying, 'I'm really tired. Good night, then.'

He closed his eyes and saw Gilly and her bent hands. He knew she'd be there all night, so he didn't speak when Johnny lay trembling beside him. But afterwards Johnny said, 'This is love, you know,' and Tom thought, 'God.

A genuine queer.' In the morning he took the Tube to Brixton, knocking on doors along Canterbury Crescent until he found the top-floor room, and didn't see Johnny for months.

He liked the squat. Every dole day was a celebration in the pub by the viaduct, a big room with bare boards, a pool table, and a hot square of sunlight through the open doors, Tom round-shouldered over his pint, short of small-talk but always good for a loan from his car-repair work, making lumpy roll-ups in brown cigarette paper, brushing the spilled tobacco off his lap, watching the students and hippies, his eyebrows high and pointed, thinking, 'London.' Then he'd head to the squat and sit on a tyre under the apple tree, a bottle of wine in a bucket, giving his downward smile as people drifted over with their dope.

And at night he was cosy in the thin sleeping bag that he'd bought from a hippy for a couple of joints. The hippy called it a doss bag, and was angry, holding up the joints, saying, 'They're nature's gift, man. Nature's gift.' But then it got cold, and Tom was still fixing cars in the gutter, rain in his toolbox, kids stealing bits, and afterwards the owners giving him hell, though it was a great way to pick up work. Sometimes he could test the cars, so he'd park and stare at women or cruise at 4 a.m., London empty as a street map, stopping at skips and finding an office chair, a table, and the big old electric fire. Then he changed the brake pads on a Mark II Golf which stopped in Chiswick on its test drive, a front wheel jammed, traffic backed up to the flyover so that the breakdown truck couldn't get through, and Tom sitting next to the owner till the swearing drove him out, forgetting his BMW tools, nothing left but a penknife.

On Christmas Eve he started home. He phoned from Victoria Bus Station, giving the ETA, but his dad said, 'It's a long way. You don't have to come.'

'I want to,' said Tom.

'Yes, but I'm saying it's not necessary. We're all right, you know. And Gilly gets over-excited.'

So he went back to the squat. He'd left the fire on, why not, but shivered all day, the doss bag round his shoulders, the phone as cold as a conch when he went to the box across the road to call his dad who said, 'Well, it is a long way. Too far, really.'

He met a painter in the dole queue, but their first job was a house in a terrace and Tom went round the back and sanded the wrong windows, everyone amazingly angry. The squatters' pub was too cheerful, so he spent his dole in a losers' boozer round the corner, alone with the lonely old men, neatly spaced around the room. At last even they were too much. All that winter – bored, sober, cold, un-stoned – he went nowhere but the dole and the Paki paper shop, living off chocolate, crisps, and cola, staring into cars but too depressed to steal, scratching up dog-ends frozen to the ground and smoking them off a pin, re-rolling the tarry stubs. He spent his seventeenth birthday coughing over the big electric fire thinking, 'When I get money I'll buy a coat and a scarf and a hat,' but knowing he wouldn't. Then Johnny was in his doorway.

'How did you find me?'

'Mac came round.'

'He was in London?'

'His job placement. Some sort of office or sales thing. Sounds awful.' He giggled, his face pink from the cold, a new floppy haircut, his long coat open, a scarf to his knees. He strode to the window, elaborately casual. 'And why did anyone ever listen to him, Tom? Really, I still wonder. His cheap suit, like some kind of minor mafioso. And he's going to be *very* fat and greasy. May hated him. We sent him away, I'm afraid. We gave him a cup of tea in the kitchen while he made all kinds of smirking remarks, some about me, some about May, some about you, then I said it was a terrible shame but we were so busy. How people change. Him *and* us.

'Anyway,' looking out of the cracked window, 'I wondered if you wanted a job. Clearly you can't stay here. And we've so much work at my dad's. I suppose, at great expense and inconvenience, we might even find you a room.' His T-shirt said, 'We love happy time life!'

Tom took the job, but stayed at the squat till he moved into May's room, working through her China books, his nose tickled by the tassels on her Chinese quilt on the bed that maybe didn't squeak, and in those days his dreams were fine.

12

A witch stole the shadows of the villagers. Her name was May. She lived with the shadows at the bottom of the river. She made them stand around crops to kill them, or around a man so that he was blind, or around herself so that she had the cover of night.

Without their shadows the villagers were weightless.

One villager fell in love with himself so that his come squirted inwards and his belly swelled with a baby that ate him inside.

Another made his sons work till they were old enough to argue, then killed them. One day his youngest son found skeletons in the field. He said, 'Were these my brothers, who've disappeared?' His father said, 'No, these were women. See, they have no dick bone.' When the boy was older he said, 'Father, there's no such thing as a dick bone,' so his father killed him.

Another was so lonely that he went out when it was windy, so that the wind could take his arm. Or he stood with his eyes closed so the wind pressed against him, cheek to cheek. A woman said hello but he punched her, saying, 'You're blocking the wind.'

The punch took out her eye, and no one would love her until a good man bought her a glass eye. But one day a pretty boy walked past and the glass eye swivelled after him so the man punched her and the eye fell out and the man stamped it to bits. The woman put a rag in the socket and stayed at home cursing the pretty boy, who fell ill. His sweetheart cut off her foot to make broth, and the boy got better and said, 'What good is a girl with one foot?' But a kind boy courted the girl and she set him tasks to win her and he did them all and at last she said, 'Count every hair on my body and I'll marry you.' Laughing, he counted them but by the end he didn't love her, so the girl threw herself in the river.

Before she drowned she said, 'A witch is here.' So now the villagers knew where their shadows were. They dragged the witch from the river but it was dawn and their shadows were tall and drove them away. They went back at noon and killed the witch, and their small shadows crept back under them.

But now the villagers could only go to their fields at noon. They grew poor and moved away and the village died and people said it was the curse of the murdered witch.

13

Tom got there early, but they were ready at the pub table, shoulder to shoulder. 'Hello, Charlie,' he said.

The girlfriend said, 'And I'm Alice,' frowning at Tom, who was not to be trusted.

Tom said, 'Seen Mac?'

'We've seen nobody, have we, Charles. We stay in and study.'

'Well, usually.'

'We wondered what you were doing, Tom. Are you working, for instance?'

'What about Johnny? Seen him?'

Charlie said, 'He called me.'

'No!' said Alice, shocked.

'How can I stop people phoning, honey?' His greasy blond hair, acne pits, melted nose: a sick lion's face.

Tom said, 'What did he say? Anything about his dad?'

'No. It was like, just a chat. He said did I fancy meeting up, but . . .'

'You didn't want to.'

'Well, we're really busy, you know.'

'How was he?'

'People can phone,' said Alice. 'Yes. But you needn't encourage them.'

'He was OK, I think,' said Charlie. 'Hated college,

that's all. I wanted to meet up, you know, but there's all these lectures and essays and stuff.' Where did he come from, anyway? Somewhere boring. Fading into his background. 'Terrible, what you said on the phone. If I'd known.'

At last a wary glance at Tom, who said, 'His bastard dad.'

'These Third World fathers,' said Alice. She sighed: 'My glass is empty, Honeybuns,' and Charlie headed for the bar. To Tom: 'We always say "Honeybuns".'

Tom folded his arms.

She said, 'Charles tells me everything, you see. Everything. He wants to put all that behind him: Mac and the old folks' place and everything. He's had enough. He wants a normal life. Normal, you see. Do you want to be normal?'

'I do,' he said, surprised.

'It's Mac we should be careful about. Your beloved leader. And he was with Johnny, you know.'

'What? When?'

Alice, plain and simple, pursed her lips. 'I've said too much. I didn't want to get into this. We discussed it this morning and last night. We decided to keep out of the whole thing. You should as well.'

Tom looked round: hurry up, Charlie.

She said, 'You seem very straightforward, Tom. A friend of mine always says, "If you find anyone else like Charles." But I always say, "Charles and I are permanent." She's really nice. Annie. I'll give you her number.'

She looked at him again, her pencil poised, suddenly dubious: 'She'll insist on changes, Tom. I warn you.'

Charlie sat down with an old man's grunt. 'I'm just writing down Annie's number. You remember Annie, Honeybuns.'

A flicker of fear in Charlie's eyes, and Tom said, 'What's this about Mac and Johnny?'

'Christ, Tom. I mean you should ask him. How should I know?' A nervous laugh: 'God, you look bad. Been fighting or something?'

'I can't sleep.'

'We're engaged,' said Alice. 'Tell him, Charles.'

Tom stood up. 'Have a fine time, OK,' and he was out the door with Charlie after him, Alice tangled in her chair and the table and her bag of books.

Charlie on the pavement: 'Tom, I forgot: this woman phoned. Ellie, I think she said.' He looked back at Alice, heading their way. 'We're not really engaged. Not a hundred per cent. She's all right, you know. You've seen the worst of her. Understandable. But come round if you want. You could do with a shower maybe.' With a gulp: 'When Alice is out, obviously.'

'Oh, Tom. Thank goodness you've called. Wherever have you been? We've tried everywhere. That takeaway place, as well. Nobody knew. I mean you'd vanished.'

Tom in a call box off the Whitechapel Road, holding the phone next to his hair or his cheek or away from him, because Ellie is a friend of his dad.

'But never mind, Tom. You've called. That's the main thing. You don't remember me, I suppose, but I've seen you. You came to the service, that day, in the summer-house, last year. I used to help your daddy. He helped me, you see, with my late husband. Alfred. Alfred left me. He was ill, I think, already. Now I look back I think it made him a bit short-tempered perhaps, so I don't bear a grudge and your father helped me to see that.

'Anyway, water under the bridge. But listen: Gillian is fine. The council took her. A very nice lady. She's in a special home, or a special school I mean. I'll get the number. My friend says it's very, very nice. If you ask me, if you don't mind me saying, she perhaps could have gone sooner. I'm not saying anything against Mr Lawson, your father, goodness knows, but.

'So Gillian is all right. And your daddy too, really. I mean it's all in hand, Tom. It is Tom, isn't it?

'So anyway. How it happened. I went to your house, or your daddy's house, that Saturday, as usual, for the washing and hoovering. But nobody answered. I was worried right away. I mean, Gillian was in the window as usual, but she didn't look right. And your daddy, where was he?

'And he's been a bit strange, as you know. We used to go for lunch every Saturday, while the washing was in the machine, just to a cafe locally. Your dad paid. Gillian really liked it, and they didn't mind her, which was very nice, the wheelchair and so on. But then your dad started. The worst thing was the singing. But also he was going over to other people, standing right next to them, and watching them. I said, "Peter. Really," and eventually he'd come away, but he didn't want to. He looked like my Alfred, the same attitude. Angry. He wanted to watch them eating.

'And even if he didn't do that, he'd do this other thing. He'd be sat with you but not really listening. He'd be twitchy and turning round, and you knew there'd be trouble. Then all of a sudden he was off. He'd go to one of the customers or the girl behind the counter, all polite, and tell them their collar was crooked, or their shoes were tied wrong, or the little tab – you know what I mean, at the back of your sweater, that little nylon tab thing inside the neck? – he'd say it was sticking out, and "Shall I put it back?" His hands all twitchy. He couldn't help it. It drove him mad. You didn't know whether to laugh or what.

'So we stopped going. It was too stressful. I'd worry all week, if they'd turn us away or what would happen. And the singing. Just bursting out, really loud. Hymns or songs or just la-la-la. So I said, "Well, I'll make us a nice lunch at home." Chips and things, which Gilly liked.

'But then, on the Saturday, no answer. I had a key because sometimes I had to pop out for things, and your father said, you know, take this. So eventually I go in. Nobody. And Gillian, so distressed. Not clean. I said, "It's all right, Gilly."

'But nobody downstairs. Well, I shouted and called. I didn't want to go upstairs, but I thought, "You can't call the police, just for that." I had to go.

'He was in the bathroom. I didn't fancy that at all. I

mean, no offence, but going into the bathroom after him. But who else would do it? He was sitting on the bath: the edge, like. He was stuck. He didn't know what to do. My daughter laughed when I said. I said, "You weren't there, lady."

'He had a tube of toothpaste in one hand, the top off, and a razor in the other hand. One of those disposables. But he'd put toothpaste on the razor. So now he was stuck.

'I went straight downstairs. I called Mrs Figgis, my friend. Thank goodness she was in. Usually she goes to the hospice on Saturdays, a very nice lady, so kind. But before that she worked for the council. Donkey's years, actually. So she arranged everything. A nice lady came and then an ambulance for both of them, Gillian and Mr Lawson, your father.

'But listen, Tom: the housing officer has been round already. They've got a waiting list for council houses, you know. But I said, "Well, he has to clear the house." You, I mean. Because there's all the furniture and your father's belongings, and perhaps some things of yours and Gillian's, though the lady from the special school or whatever it is, she took Gillian's clothes and things, as far as I can see. And I suppose there's the bills to settle, the final bills and whatnot.

'And also, the other thing, his assistant or whatever he is. Darren. You met him, I think. He wants money. "Compensation". I won't say what for. You can talk to him. I said to my daughter, "Tom's more his age, so they can talk, can't they."

'So that's what's happened. I'm very sorry to tell you, Tom. And then you didn't call. And I tried to find Mrs Lawson, your mum, but of course she went to Spain, and nobody's heard for years. So unless you've heard from her . . .

'Anyway, I'll get the number. And the number for the place for Gillian. And the gentleman in the Housing Department. But at least you've got in touch now, so we can start making some, you know, progress.

'Tom? Are you there?'

'Yes.'

'All right. So. Anyway, I'll get those numbers. Hang on while I go. Now where's my glasses?'

Very slowly Tom put the phone down, quietly so no one would hear.

14

Tom saw a river. Its water was so clear that strangers thought they were walking in a cold wind and were drowned.

He lay breathing the van smells. He was stiff and straight in the doss bag, staring up in the dark. 'Calm down, for Christ's sake.'

The river ran through a forest. The forest was beautiful and full of food, with birds like lamps, and leopards that were really ghosts.

Street noise outside. The early evening traffic through the dark, and he was sick with dread about Dad and Gillian and Johnny and May.

He saw a little boy. The boy lived in a village but roamed the forest all day, hunting and playing and collecting wood.

Tom tucked the doss bag tighter round his neck, thinking, 'Please, a decent story. Just me and May.'

So Tom was the boy in the forest. He looked at the high trees, and the sunlight filtering through, and sang as he walked.

In the van, Tom thought, 'Where's May?'

The boy had a friend. Every day they wandered the forest, climbing the trees for fruit and eggs, and stealing honey from the forest bee, the deadliest creature in these hills. Her name was May.

So Tom was climbing a tree. He looked across and there was May, her hair in a ragged crop, her dusty pretty feet. They'd found a nest, as they found nests every day. She peeped inside and gave him her little girl's grin. She lifted out a speckled egg and put it with a careful frown in the bosom of her dress. Every day she went home with eggs, although her father was rich.

One day she went home with a leech on her precious part.

'Christ.'

Her father was angry, and asked about her life with the boy. She said, 'When I'm eight we'll be married.' And she talked of their adventures in the forest, and how the boy helped with her makeup, and how she likewise spread the white paste on his face, with a dab of crimson on the lips, and oil to make the hair shine, so that they were alike.

But she wouldn't explain the leech. Her father blamed the boy and kept his daughter at home in his castle. But in fact the culprit was May herself, who wished to resemble the boy in every particular.

'God,' said Tom, alert in the van. 'More pervy stuff.' He lay in the dark, getting angry. 'I can change this.'

He thought: There was a river in a forest. A boy loved a girl. They were fifteen, and ready to marry. They roamed the forest, climbing for eggs and for honey from the wild bees, although the forest women told the girl, 'Do not climb,' because girls mustn't go in the trees beyond a certain age. But May sat astride the high branches and laughed at the women catching frogs in the river, or digging crabs from their burrows in the river-bank. 'Soon we'll live high up,' she said, 'and make a home with the birds.'

But May's father was a mandarin, and at last confined her in his castle. The girl pined in her rooms, and the boy pined in the forest, and when he thought of love he thought of May and held his precious part, holding it tight, because it might fall off when it was full, like May's leech.

'No, I didn't,' said Tom. 'Start again.'

There was a boy in a forest. He wanted revenge. He would kill the mandarin and marry May. He crept silently through the trees. He crept into the wind so that the prey couldn't scent him, and he squatted like a girl to piss, a stick at his member so that the water fell without sound.

'But this isn't pervy,' thought Tom. 'It's very practical. A hunter's trick.'

The mandarin was afraid of the boy, and sent two guards to kill him. But he led them to snares he'd set for pigs, then weakened them with arrows, then cut their throats, although they said, 'Don't kill us.' He left their bodies for the animals, but took armour and a sword. He polished the sword and believed it could cut the river so that the water wouldn't heal, or cut the wind, or cut today from tomorrow and make a place wide enough for a man to sit and in the morning his beard wouldn't have grown.

'But I didn't go on about this bollocks. I only thought about May, and killing her dad.'

So the boy didn't fuss with the sword. He didn't need to, because he'd win any sword fight through superior will, a wound being the outward sign of an inner division, a feminine split which the sword had merely revealed.

'Bollocks.'

The boy threw the sword away. Instead he polished the armour on the sandy bank of the river. He greased it with clarified fat, so that the plates were mirrors. He walked through the trees like swirling bits of forest and sky. His enemies would see his beauty, and their own image in the armour, and would fail because they were ugly.

'No, they wouldn't.'

The boy threw the armour in a stream. He walked through the forest, thinking only about May and her father and unarmed combat. He hung a bundle of palm leaves against a tree, punching for weeks until he punched the tree. He practised the following throws and holds: climbing rabbit bites the eagle; oil on the swan's neck; and small fish confronts the waterfall but fails until the sixth attempt. He hid his testicles, lifting them into his belly with tight cloths. He checked often that his loins were empty.

'Enough,' said Tom. 'I'll be the mandarin.'

This mandarin came from London. He was kind. He gave food to the local people. He sheltered them when the river flooded, and they loved him, although his wife had smiled at a pretty boy so that he cast her out to be a beggar in the mountains, first cutting off her lips so that she smiled at everyone.

'No.'

The mandarin had never married. He was in love with May, who was a poor girl from a forest village. He came from San Francisco. He'd been raised in a single Chinatown room, the children sharing a bed, brothers and sisters lying feet to faces, to prevent mischief. This might explain some later matters. He worked in a Chinese bank on Mission Street, but in the evenings he wore a white linen suit, his hair slicked back, and loitered in opium houses with other wastrels. He became an addict. In his weakness he couldn't service his harlots and was ashamed and then angry. He saw among the opium smoke that a man's place was that great swath of the earth from Turkey to China, where he might stand berobed with legs wide, his women crouching. One day, in a house by the docks, the opium master was himself smoking, so that his woman came from a back room. Her bound feet entered the young man's dreams: he would fill his house with women who tottered from room to room, or rested against the furniture like swimmers, and he would be the lord. So he stole from the bank and came to China, staring from the ship's rail at the Canton waterfront, rapt with desire at the lovely cripples, and nothing else would do.

In the van, Tom watched the mandarin with suspicion. But he also thought how a bound foot would fit in your hand.

The mandarin found a castle in a forest where poor

women could be bought. He clothed them in a stiff wig and a thick embroidered coat, laughing at their peasant surprise, and caused their feet to be bound. They were pleased by their new feet, thinking themselves like fine ladies, and he bowed his head over the white silk stockings and red silk slippers and the toes bent under. When he was weary of them, he thought how they couldn't return to the forest and the fields, and he wept for them, as they also wept.

'What's going on?' thought Tom.

One day a girl came to the castle with honeycomb to sell. The mandarin said, 'I will train you in the ways of ladies.' He gave her a heavy wig, and a heavy gown that was stiff with needlework. He smiled and said, 'A true gentlewoman must have bound feet,' and he showed her the silk ribbons which are tightened until the toes fold under and touch the heels. 'I wonder what binding would suit you. Perhaps "the bow" or "the new moon".' Her name was May.

'God,' thought Tom.

The mandarin felt a stab of pity. Perhaps he should give up his dream. But then he thought of the beauty of bound feet and became full of tenderness, saying, 'The finer the lady the more becoming are bound feet.'

May said, 'The love of bound feet is the love of a woman humbled.'

'It is the love of beauty,' said the mandarin, 'and the desire that the beloved should be perfect.'

May said, 'Besides the pain there is an impeding of the blood, so that the toes are mortified and fall off.

Degenerate men may call them "crescent moons", "three-inch golden lotuses", and "curved lotuses to fill a hand", yet the feet are rotten in their red silk slippers and white silk stockings.'

'Won't you do this for me?' said the mandarin. 'Surely the greater the sacrifice the greater the love.'

'I only want freedom.'

'But why should you wish for freedom, when freedom means departure from one who will adore you?'

May didn't reply. She only thought how the forest paths would be hard for her and the trees impossible, and only the castle would remain. Nevertheless she went every day to his rooms, where he knelt and snatched her feet into his lap. 'Tighter,' he said. 'Bind them tighter.'

'Bastard,' thought Tom. But he also thought of a lover whose feet were small, like the feet of a child in the forest.

Now May staggered from chair to chair. How the mandarin greeted her new feet! He knelt on the floor and drew them to him, his head in her lap, his silk cap slipping off and the oiled pigtail spilling out, and she stroked his head, so that he seemed like her own child.

'Your feet are like the hooves of a deer,' he said, 'one of the tiny deer of the forest, which are as high as a man's knee, and wait in a snare, shivering and thin, trembling when the hunter comes, who will kill it with a single blow, though first taking his pleasure, whether it be doe or buck.'

One day the mandarin was delayed and May sat in his anteroom. She would be happy among his orchids and silk, she thought, and the plates that could be laid on a book and the book still read. And she half admired him for spurning the functions of woman and man.

'No she didn't,' said Tom.

May was a healthy girl. She wanted a normal life. Normal. And now she saw a shrivelled thing in a silver frame and thought, 'His wife's lips.'

'God,' thought Tom, and remembered the boy in the forest.

This boy had been faithful, despite his faults, and raged against the mandarin, who was crippling his love. And at night in the hot forest he thought of May in those private moments when we are hermaphrodite.

'Christ.'

But there was no time to lose, so Tom put the boy at the castle gates. His precious parts were bound up, which was fair and reasonable and good tactics, but the guards searched him, their hands between his legs, and laughed with surprise, saying, 'This is a woman.' So the boy killed them, the bow leaping to his hand.

The stairs to the mandarin's rooms were steep. Their treads sloped outwards and were narrow and slick with wax and designed to creak. But the boy had spent his life in the trees. He braced against the walls and climbed without touching the steps. Then he heard May shriek and knew that the story was working itself through.

She had peeked around a door and found the mandarin's bed.

She had gone to the bed and fingered its coverlet of silk.

She had pulled back the coverlet, and stopped in surprise. Along the pillow was a row of wigs, like her own wig.

She had pulled back the sheet. Below each wig was a coat, like her own embroidered coat.

There was a gap amid the coats. It was just big enough for the mandarin to lie in.

She drew down the sheet. Below each coat was a pair of legs. They were severed at the knee. A leg fell to the floor, pretty in its white stocking and red slipper, and seemed to kick her.

Now the mandarin rushed in, his little sword a blur, and Tom said, 'God,' the story unstoppable.

But the boy was also there. He burst into the bedroom, his bow humming. The mandarin fell with arrows in his face.

But where was May? Now Tom saw her. She stumbled towards him, her face blank. Why was she on her knees? She laid her hand on the table, looking at him with a dumb appeal, and the story had won.

The boy gathered her up. He carried her away and never left her till her wounds were dry. She lived with him in the deepest part of the forest, and bore her affliction bravely, but often looked at the sunlit paths among the trees, which she had loved so well.

15

Tom was walking fast, clearing his head. A stupid sick dream, the worst yet. He strode around the block and back to the van, then around the block again, kicking walls because the dream had beaten him.

Bollocks to the dreams. But how else could he be with May? He got into the driver's seat, the doss bag spread on his lap. Three a.m. The world is speaking Chinese.

And here was another thing: with every dream the river got bigger. At first it had been a torrent among mountains, and the girl saying, 'I'm young and lovely, as you see.' Then it was broad and fast below the black cliff, and now it was slow and wide among forests, as if the stories were heading downstream, getting closer.

He sat very still in the cold van, his muscles tense instead of shivering. 'It's because there's no draughts in a car, except if you make your own.' Tense and cold, he wouldn't turn his head, so the night gathered round him. The Whitechapel Road was quiet under the street lights, asleep but its eyes open, and he thought about the age of China and its millions of dead: scalded and strangled and shot, or stoned to death or fallen off cliffs, or choked on noodles or tripping over a dog, but above all death by knife and fire.

He remembered when he last saw Johnny.

He'd been pubbing in Brixton. He'd walked very carefully from the Whitechapel Tube, a secretive grin, past the hospital, round behind the takeaway, through bin bags and empty cardboard boxes into the kitchen, and had sat at the steel table, drunk and stoned, watching Johnny make toast, pleasantly bemused at his weird haste as he stacked the slices. Now Tom suddenly understood: 'It's because toast is an insulator.'

Medicine was disgusting, said Johnny, so maybe he'd write about the Chinese abroad. You could do the history of a house, maybe this house, and the people who'd lived here, going back through the generations to China.

'Not that rap crap?' said Tom.

'Well, you know. Maybe someone could do the music.'

And he was still damn fast with the toast, leaning from the hips, his long narrow back, swiftly spreading marge, then the knife deep in the jam so that it covered the toast in one quick sweep and a couple of fiddles at the corners. Tom nodded at the windscreen: margarine and jam are also insulators.

Johnny turned off the grill and relaxed a bit. The lid of the margarine tub was upside down on the table. He lifted the tub at one end, slackly between finger and thumb so that it turned upside down, and pressed it into the lid. He let it spin upright and put it in the fridge, swiftly so the cold couldn't get out. Fag fussing.

'My dad's trying something new on the menu. It's rack of lamb.'

'Don't.'

'He was going to do ram instead of lamb. But there's a lack of ram.'

His hair was greased straight back. A thin black tie over a silk shirt, the sleeves rolled up, slim slick arms like a shop dummy. His pants were baggy linen: his linen jacket on a chair back. Now Tom recognized the look: a Shanghai gangster, circa 1920. Fag vanity.

Johnny put the lid on the jam jar and turned it the wrong way. When the ends of the threads clicked he turned it the right way: this prevents cross-threading. He held the sugar bowl over the cups, moving it aside to empty the spoon. He poured the kettle, following the tea bags for maximum infusion. He added milk while the water still swirled, and stirred vertically so the sugar didn't just circle the bottom. White scalp through his hair, which was countable like a wig: they have hairs not hair.

'How's my sister? I never see her nowadays. Or you – though I hear you, of course.' A squirm and a kind of frowning smirk: 'Not what I expected when I offered you the job.'

'Blimey, Johnny. I mean.'

'I came to the squat, at great personal inconvenience.'

He halved the toast into faggot triangles and brought it all to the table. Straight-backed he prodded the toast with his face turned away, lifted it with his fingertips, bit, his lips held clear, then looked at the bite. Tom saw May in him, but soured with loneliness, fussy where she's quick.

'We might be going to China,' said Tom. 'Me and May. Tracing her roots. Up that river, you know.'

'Maybe I'll come. They're my roots too.'

'I thought you didn't fancy the place,' said Tom. 'Third World toilets and all that.' Deliberately he said, 'Anyway, it'd be me and May – a boyfriend–girlfriend thing, you know.'

'China,' said Johnny, stiff-backed. 'Yes, you're welcome.' But he was very hurt. He slid the cup towards him, then off the table edge, then lifted it, thus needing the minimum of tricky balancing. 'I could do so much,' he said, 'given time.'

Tom was crouched behind a parked car. He was watching Mr Tan on the tall stool behind the counter, staring up stupefied at the TV on the wall. At eleven o'clock Tan came through the counter flap and turned the sign to Closed.

Tom waited, then went round the back. He took a deep breath and opened the kitchen door. 'My god,' said Wei.

They were at the steel table, Wei astonished, Mr Tan in his chef's whites, sleeves pushed to the elbows, his thick smooth arms on a played-out game of Patience. He saw Tom and went grey.

'Mr Tan. I very sorry. Sorry about Johnny.'

Tan glanced down at the cards. He looked up and said, 'Go, please.'

'Yes. Definitely. I just want to say I very, very sorry.'

'Go.' Tan's fists were bunched on the table, muscles moving in his slick arms.

'Yes. Definitely. But, one thing. I just, I mean I dream

about China.' A nervous laugh. 'Maybe you have medicine. Tiger bits or bear's feet. You know.'

'Not understand. Waste of time,' said Tan, lifting his barmaid arms and dropping them back, Tom watching the buttery lumps of muscles so that he lost the thread.

'I mean. Mr Tan. I very ill. I not sleep.'

'Talk English!'

'Yes. Sorry. I mean I'm dreaming about a river. Does that make sense?'

Mr Tan stared, his bull-dyke forearms still at last: 'Johnny is dead.'

Tom bowed his head. 'I very sorry. Really. Is unbelievable.'

'English!'

'Yes. I wish I spoke Cantonese, Mr Tan.'

'You not Cantonese. Not Chinese. Not a man!'

'What? What you mean?'

'English! You English, you talk English.'

'Yes. OK. No problem.'

Tan's fingers curled, holding some outrage. 'Dirty. A dog.'

'No. Wait. Just a minute.'

'Go. Where my bike?'

'It stolen. It is stolen. It was stolen. It has been stolen.'

'You are really very useless.'

'Yes. But that other thing. I mean it was nothing. It didn't matter. Anyway it was somebody else. This other friend, who . . .'

'Go now.' Tan's hand, smooth as a glove, over his eyes.

'What about May?'

'What?'

'I dream about her, so I want to talk to her and still see her.'

'Bastard! Talk to May, you finished.'

'Look,' said Tom, pointing. 'About May. You split us up. I don't want any more of that crap.'

Tan got up, his arms curved. Tom said, 'Look, you fat fool. Johnny is dead because of you. It's your fault, OK? And I'm going to marry May.'

Afterwards he thought, 'When they say that a man is strong, that's what it means.' His fingers crushed together behind his back, Tan's other hand on his neck, he was pitched into the alley as Wei held the door and bowed him out with a grin.

Tom stumbled to the Whitechapel Road, Wei laughing and following in the rain.

'I'm OK,' said Tom. 'I'm fine. Didn't want to hurt him, that's all, my future father-in-law.'

'What?'

'My wife's father.'

'Ah. Good. Congratulations.'

'What you want?'

'Bike, please.'

Tom got in the van. 'Tell Mr Tan that I keep dreaming about May. It means I'm going to marry her.'

'Yes,' said Wei, laughing. 'Yes. Dreams about May. And you tell Mr Tan.'

'It's nothing bad, OK.'

'You tell her father!'

'Little shit.'

Wei holding the van door, sympathetic for once. 'Tom, forget this place. Really. Nothing here for you.'

Tom started the engine. 'How did Mr Tan . . . I mean, who told him about Johnny? Was it somebody called Mac?'

But Wei only shrugged and grinned.

'Little Chinky shit.'

16

Tom waited in the doss bag in the driver's seat in a side road near the takeaway, hot with shame. 'No wonder May dumped me.'

He needed Tan asleep and then he'd climb to May's room and wait for ever if he had to. 'Hurry up, you flabby bastard.'

He pictured Mr Tan, his slippers flapping on curly lino or fat-spattered tiles or restless under the table, his bare arms on the playing cards. Tan shuffled to the sink, his fingers spread because they were fat and sweaty, and slid the fake Rolex up his arm on its expanding metal bracelet, which you can only do with bald arms, and rinsed the last pots with his piggy hands.

Midnight. Tom saw him with a clipboard in the stockroom under the stairs, the dog snorting through the tongue-and-groove wall from the shed next door, and he was thinking about the boy who soiled his daughter: 'You poyfriend? Poyfriend?'

Tan frowned over his glasses. His feet hurt. He'd lost a kilo of rice, because all cooks are thieves.

He imagined long talks with his son, but now it was too late. He thought:

I found your mother on a hot day. First my parents died and then I sold the land for too little to a grinning uncle and came by luck to the wife fair, money in my pocket, the women in their underclothes, and I bought her from curiosity not desire and because it was a day for doing anything.

This was in the mountains near Tibet. She blushed because I was young like her. Her father was drunk. I haggled and was told a price and walked away.

I was eating and looking at the other women, who were older than me. Really I thought they were sexy and older. But she had blushed and shivered so I dropped the food and went to her father again, in a hurry but looking calm. A fat old farmer was arguing. I pushed him away and put money in her father's hand and he said, 'This old man will pay more.'

I gave him more money. He said, 'The old man will pay more still.' I said, 'No,' and told the girl, 'I've bought you.' She cried and got dressed and we walked straight off the market and down the road, the girl looking back until the road went round a hill.

We sat down, just out of sight. Men were putting wheat on the road. She sat and cried and I watched the men. They were spreading wheat on the tar. I watched for a while because they sometimes ran in front of carts and made them go around the grain. I saw it was because wooden or iron wheels, and the hooves of buffalo, were too hard and turned the grain to dust. But people or rubber tyres were just hard enough, so the wheat was threshed. I'm always interested in things.

We went to the river and got a boat. The bunks were this far apart and there were a hundred people in that boat but I climbed into her bunk when the lights went out. Someone said, 'There are children,' but I didn't care. She cried and this was sexy. I don't say this because it's right; just to tell you. She was helpless.

I was angry so I didn't talk, thinking that I was rich but not free, or that I was rich so any woman would have me without payment. I was young and stupid. But I spilt food on my shirt and she laughed. She said, 'You're like my brother, and I always laughed at him.' I liked her to mock me.

Then she had you two, and I hired a midwife and bought foreign baby clothes and rented a good house and bought a crib that we left when we went downstream.

We always went downstream. We got to the coast and your mother worked in a factory and I built more factories, digging drains. But she never got well. I bought folk cures and was a porter or river coolie or a bodyguard.

Then we heard about the doctors in Hong Kong, so we crept at night through marshes to the English fence, hiding while the little Gurkhas went by, you two drugged, then over with people we never saw again except for the guide who took the last of my money and said, 'It's not enough.'

I worked for him for a year, and your mother died. I brought more people over the fence. I slept in fields near the fence. You slept in restaurants, in the pantry. Once you slept on TVs stolen from the docks. Lots of brown boxes in a room with no windows. And once you stayed in a brothel. The mats were very dirty, so I moved you. You had a lot of mothers!

All that time I worked at the fence. I knew that fence! One time a boy hung on the wire by his neck, so we carried him into Hong Kong, his mother calling his soul to come back. Another time . . .

That fence was my life. One day I'll go back. But maybe it's different, now the English have gone.

We sent people to London. That was easy: we put them on a boat or a plane. There were other things too, sending people to Japan. And things with money-changing and some of the money stuck to my hands so I bought factory-made shoes.

Yes, I told you before. I was proud of the factory shoes. I said, 'I'll never wear handmade shoes again!'

'Oh, Daddy,' you said. So English, such an English little boy. And I told you about London, when you were babies and I didn't know anything and I thought, 'Can an English phone understand Cantonese?'

Yes, I know: 'Oh, Daddy.'

So I picked a lucky day and brought you to London. I didn't tell the snakehead. We were poor. Then I was a debt-collector for the London snakehead. See this scar? A woman threw a dish.

Then I was a cook. Then I came here. I was a cook, but then the manager left because we argued, so I was the manager. I was glad he left. I made him leave.

Then when you were older the snakehead had a tax thing so my name is on the deeds, though really I'm only the manager, so the takeaway isn't ours.

I did all this for you.

*

Mr Tan, that flat-footed quacking Cantonese, shuffled to the kitchen, Tom thinking, 'He has to shuffle to keep the slippers on.'

Tom pictured Wei and Chung at the kitchen table. They were gathering their strength to go: the Tube ride, then a bus, then the long walk to their room over a launderette in Colindale. Tan sat down, a thug Buddha, big arms making them think, 'He was with the gangs.'

Wei looked at Chung and they put on their coats. They were by the door when Tan said, 'Where are our ancestors? Did they follow us here?' He nodded at the little gilt altar in a corner. 'I bought that in London. So they didn't come with the altar. How can they find us? Who tends them? Are they tending us?'

They thought, 'This is about his son and his wife.'

Wei said, 'They find us in the end, I think.'

Tan didn't watch them leave. He got up and scraped their plates into a bowl, then checked the knobs on the big stove, because someone kept leaving the gas on. He went to the shed, grunting as he put the bowl on the floor, leftovers of leftovers, the dog trying to snuggle but he pushed it off. He sat on a box and thought of the white boy who was to blame for everything, while the dog whimpered and nuzzled, lonely too.

'You boyfriend? Boyfriend?' thought Tan, because in his head his speech was perfect. 'Beware. I am a burly beer-bellied bully-boy.'

Why was Mr Tan fat?

Raw or rare liver, veal ravioli with olive oil, broiled

or boiled or par-boiled ribs, rarebit on rye, rabbit pie, raspberry ripple, ripe pears, apple purée, bilberry or blue-berry or rhubarb roly-poly, bowls of syllabub, barrels of real ale, barrows of barley beer, lorry-loads of lovely bubbly, and a liberal lollypop allowance, so he was a plump bulbous blubbery blob lobbed over the barbed-wire barrier into imperial Albion.

'Johnny,' thought Tom. 'It's Johnny saying this.'

A bandit attacked Master Tan, who gently held him, saying, 'You tried to hurt yourself and I stopped you.'

Master Tan was so wise that he grew rich. He put away his loincloth and bought trousers, the first in the village, but was too lazy to button the flies. He bought factory cigarettes and struck poses from the advertising posters. He stared shrewdly through the smoke, and practised many methods for flicking off the ash. He held the cigarette near his ear or casually in his cupped fist. But he was used to the long village pipes so the smoke went up his nose.

Master Tan gave so little impediment to his food that he needn't wipe his lips or his arse. He gave so little impediment to his drink that he drank without swallow-ing and pissed without afterwards shaking his dick.

Master Tan said, 'Contemplate towers not wells. Stand on bridges when boats go under. Buy a caged bird and observe its belly. Tom, if personal circumstances permit, go to fishing villages where boats are onshore. If a boat is raised on stilts to be painted, then this is worth a two-day walk. Consider birds and boats and pretty girls, sustained by a shape.'

Master Tan's pupil said, 'I want to be happy.' The Master replied, 'I want to live only in the right-hand side of the world.' All day he leapt to the right but when he was tired his left side was still there. So he lay on his left side, to control it, and this was in a cellar with cold walls.

Master Tan placated the North Dragon, which makes earthquakes. He scheduled the planting of the rice. He made kites and predicted floods. He built an outhouse where the wind turned round and round like a dog and at last slept.

Master Tan's wife and son died and his daughter loved a foreigner. He sang, 'The elephant's foot / Is soft-hard as the wheels of a bus, / His shits as big as boxing gloves. / Still, as she runs between, / The little mouse says: "Me! Me! Me!"' – but he was still lonely.

In the van, Tom thought:

Maybe there was a one-child policy in those days, so one of the twins would go for adoption. Or perhaps twins were ill-luck, especially boy-girl twins because the girl's virtue was tainted in the womb. Or maybe the tribe hated twins, because only animals have multiple births, and so one of the children must be killed, just as a child is killed if it's crippled, or the parents have too many children, or too many children of that sex, or if a sibling is still suckling, or if the parents are ill, as a mother might be ill if she has twins and wonders which should die, twisting in her fingers the leaf she will push down its throat. Or perhaps Mr Tan said, 'In Hong Kong they have so much food that you shit every day, sometimes twice, although their nasty toilets are indoors.'

Anyway, they left China, crossing the marsh at night, and the babies were first over the barbed wire, then Mr Tan thinking, 'Certainly, in crossing a fence, a man knows when he passes halfway,' then his wife thinking, 'They can see up my skirt,' dying but she didn't know, and this was their unknown mother, never discussed, long since lost in China.

What does Mr Tan, brave but bereaved, want for May?

The belle of the ball in Ralph-Lauren-label bridal apparel, pearl earrings, a valuable veil, and something borrowed, something blue, arriving at a bar or club lobby or pub parlour in a Volvo, Rover, or Roller (lily-of-the-valley on the wireless aerial and rear-view mirror), with lobelias available for every reveller's lapel, while a big brass band plays Ravel's Bolero, 'Lilliburlero', 'Roll Over, Beethoven', 'The Old Bull and Bush', 'Bye-bye, Blackbird', 'My Love is Like a Red Red Rose' by Robbie Burns, 'The Red Red Robin Comes Bob-bob-bobbing Along', and airs and lays of popular appeal.

In his sleep, Tom thought, 'Shut up, Johnny.'

Then leaving by private plane with her loyal, reliable, valorous, and very virile beloved (a libel lawyer or airline pilot or Riviera playboy or a billionaire big in railways, breweries, and ball bearings) for Elba, Alba, Bali, Bari, Bora-Bora, Balboa, Bilbao, or the Hôtel Louvre-Rivoli on the Rue de la République, then home to their lovely villa (rented or lent or let; urban, suburban or rural), living the life of Riley in a royal London borough with Larry, Laurie, Louie, Errol, Earl, Eli, Ellery, Oliver, Ivor, Rory, Raoul, Barry, Blair, Burl and Billy-Bob, their lively bilingual baby boys.

'Enough, Johnny,' said Tom.

Mr Tan turned off the kitchen light and went upstairs. He didn't undress any more. He kicked off the slippers and pulled the quilt over him. He wanted to talk to May but she was on nights.

He frowned as he fell asleep. He was trying to understand the river, which flowed here from China. He thought, 'I'm asleep in the bedroom above the takeaway in the Whitechapel Road,' but he frowned because the river had run over rapids, under houses on stilts, yet now passed Chelsea and the Isle of Dogs.

Tom thought of Tan thinking of Johnny, who was mist on the river. They saw him muddled by coal smoke, passing dirty concrete docks, through thunderous gorges, under a black cliff, and up and up to the source in the mountains near Tibet.

'Come home,' said Tan, willing his son downstream, past the pretty riverside towns, Maidenhead and Qian-jiang.

Master Tan adjusted the twelve musical tones so that yin and yang were equal. He redirected rivers so that the earth's rotation was sustained. And every day he walked through his castle and sniffed the air and said, 'The balance of happiness and unhappiness is sustained. It is good.' But in fact Tan's son was unhappy because every night a bandit climbed to Tan's daughter and made her happy.

This bandit gathered an army. Master Tan stood at his window and sniffed the air from their camp and said, 'The balance of hate and love is sustained. They will not attack.' The bandits attacked, and by as much as they hated Tan's men, by so much they laid down their lives for their friends.

So Master Tan's castle was besieged. He sniffed the air and said, 'The balance of making and breaking is sustained. We are safe.' But the bandits made ladders and broke his walls. Tan was taken, his son killed himself, and his daughter married the bandit leader. 'They won't hurt me,' said Master Tan, sniffing the prison air. But his parts were cut off while the bandit laughed.

So Master Tan roamed the hills in rags, his arms stretched out, his hands turned out at the wrists because he might just as soon cartwheel. He listened to the twelve tones, counted his fingers, put out his hand for the sky to perch on, and then lay in a cellar where drunks piss.

Finally, what does Mr Tan think of Tom?

A low-born low brow low life's by-blow, evil, violent and poor. A villain oblivious to the value of the rule of law. A layabout, vile reprobate, unbearable barbarian, ill-bred labourer, burglar and brawler, and a robber to rival Ali Baba. But above all a lover of the lower bowel and blow-jobs with the bum-boys, not ovaries, labia and vulva.

17

Tom fell onto the road. He knelt in the rain, then leaned on the van to get up.

He stood shivering, because Johnny was in his head. Two a.m. He scooped rain off the van roof and rubbed his face, then wandered through side streets, waking up, searching pavements but the dog-ends had melted. He came briefly onto the Whitechapel Road, which glittered like a river, with buildings which might or might not be black cliffs, then back to the van where he took the washing line off the door handles.

'I really, really don't fancy this.'

In the alley behind the takeaway he checked the line. It had maybe been tied to the apple tree for years, and wasn't so strong. One end held the shape of the branch. Still, it hadn't snapped when he dragged long Frank up the alley. He scratched it and fibres sprang loose.

'No choice, anyway.'

He tucked the line in the back of his belt and climbed the pipe by Johnny's window. He tied one end of the line to the pipe and climbed back down, out of breath and scuffed and his scalp itchy, but he couldn't scratch with his dirty hands. The dog barked once.

He hauled on the line and nothing broke. He tucked the end of the line into his belt and climbed to Mr Tan's room, noticing halfway up that he was cursing quietly but savagely. He pulled the line tight and grunted as he tied it round the pipe next to Tan's window, thinking of that fat rat-bastard inside and sniffing hard because maybe he could smell Marlboro.

He slid to the ground for a breather. He put his fingers under the shed door and the dog licked him then growled. Even the bastard dog hates me.

The line stretched across May's window, held by the pipes. It looked good, but it'd probably snap. He stood among the dustbins, looking up, thinking, 'I'm always doing this,' meaning that he saw holes in a plan but still went ahead.

Next to the bins was a black plastic bin bag. He kicked it, then looked inside. 'Christ.' Johnny's clothes. He dithered, then took a sweater, tying it round his head for a helmet.

He climbed the pipe next to Johnny's window. He ducked between the washing line and the wall, then stepped onto the window ledge, wanting to break in and sleep for a week.

This bit was easy, edging across Johnny's window ledge, the line behind his shoulders, gripping the window frame although his stitches hurt. But then he came to the blank wall – ten foot down to the concrete yard, and the long stride to May's window. 'Madness,' he thought, then reached a wavering leg across the drop.

'Shit!' He couldn't move. He had a foot on Johnny's window ledge, the other on May's, his hands stretched out and hooked on the two window openings, the wet washing line across his neck, his cheek pressed against London bricks.

'Bugger.' His knees shook and the stitches were bleeding. The sweater dropped over his eyes. His crotch ached.

'I'm stuck,' he said, and with a great heave pulled himself across.

He rested, sweating and cursing on May's window ledge, his breath misting the glass. Her curtains were drawn, but they always were. He couldn't see a light. He thought about tapping on the window, but instead he squinted at the latch, planning where he'd slip the knife blade. He pulled the washing line down behind his shoulders.

Where it crossed his back, up between the shoulder blades, the line broke.

Tom hung on. Spread-eagled, leaning backwards, his feet on the window ledge, his arms stretched out, he gripped the broken ends of the line. 'Shit!' The sweater fell back across his eyes.

He tapped the window with his foot, the line sliding through his hands. But his soles were rubber, not like Dad's. 'May! Are you there?'

He fell. One hand holding the line, he swung down until his feet skimmed the concrete yard. Then he went sideways through glass and wood.

His legs recovered first: he found himself high-stepping from the stockroom, tangled in glass and window frame, the dog bounding against the shed door.

He limped to the van and sat breathing hard, then

went back to the takeaway. Lights on downstairs, the dog berserk, as he took the bag of Johnny's clothes.

In the van he pulled glass from his ankle. He had an excuse to look for May at the hospital, but instead he bound the cut with one of Johnny's socks. He drove until he was lost, then sat in the dark between the street lights, the back doors open, his head on the steering wheel. After a while he saw a forest.

'Bastards. I'll burn the place down. Then they'll have to come out.'

The forest was beautiful and sloping. He walked under birches in dappled sun.

'Bollocks to them, anyway. I'll be alone and happy.'

He'd walked for hours in the forest. Alone and happy he'd eaten fruit and roots, and had drunk from tiny streams which drained the forest's gentle slope.

He knew this slope. He wouldn't go down to the valley bottom, where the ground was sodden around the river, with bushes full of biting flies, and the tribes had poison arrows and worshipped a snake. And he wouldn't go higher, where the trees thinned and there were rocky outcrops and nothing to eat except the goats of the highland folk, who leaned on their muskets watching for tigers and goat thieves. Instead he kept to this middle slope, where the trees were slim birches, and sunlight dappled onto deer-nibbled turf, and he could find the animals and plants that his tribe knew best.

'What tribe?' thought Tom.

So he remembered his village, the women with beads

and oiled hair. He'd left after a fight. He'd walked deep into the forest, keeping to this middle slope where his people had always lived.

Because of this he found the tribe's abandoned villages.

The first village was where his father had been born. In the middle was the village yard: trampled earth where still nothing grew. Around were falling huts, each with three scorched stones which had held the cooking pots of the tribe, who'd left when the animals and soil and food plants were finished. He found a hut whose roof still kept off the sun and the morning dew, and stayed for two days, digging tubers from a midden where the scraps of crops had sprouted again. Perhaps his grandparents wouldn't have hated him like his father.

Tom thought, 'What father?' He saw a man with thick arms who beat him with fists and sticks and on the last day had kicked him, so that he walked further into the forest than anyone before.

He walked on and found the village where his father's father had been a child. Decades of rain had washed its cooking stones. Its huts were fallen into piles of sticks, which were full of snakes. At the next village the huts had gone and the cooking stones were mossy.

He walked for day after day, the villages older and older, each a day's walk from the last, because a hunter will only travel half a day to his traps and half a day home, even the hunters of the ancestors' time, when men conversed with gods. He felt that he knew these men, and that he in turn was understood.

He sniffed out grubs in the deepest leaf mould, squeezing out their innards and eating as he walked. He followed monkeys by their trail of half-eaten fruit, which he gathered. He found pigs by their bitter smell and squealing young, and chewed the roots which they'd dug with their great snouts. He met a tiger that coughed and slid away, silent on the close-cropped turf.

Now the villages were hard to find, their cooking stones lost in a grassy hummock that was full of ants, its top worn flat by the forest grouse, which dances for its bride. Still he walked, looking for his tribe's first village, where the men were freshly made and wouldn't hate their sons.

'Why did my father hate me?' thought Tom. He saw a father ashamed of his son.

Now the villages had nearly vanished. On his last day he crept slowly, watching every step, hoping for the felled stump of a starch tree, or a patch of hard ground where the trees were the same age, or just a shiver down the spine because of ghosts. He was coming to the oldest village of the tribe, whose people had been wise and kind.

Instead he smelled smoke. He halted, fearing strangers. He crept on and saw a field of maize. It was tended by women he seemed to know. He crouched among bushes. At last a man appeared, half hidden under a bale of wood. The boy blinked in surprise. The man was his father.

He sat bewildered in the undergrowth. He'd left the village on the forest side, where trees came to the village edge and were kept for hunters. But he'd returned on the women's side, where the trees were cleared for crops. He stood up in the bushes till his father saw him.

This was his homecoming. His father led him to the village, punching his arm in a friendly way. But the boy was dazed, and looked around with a stranger's eye. The village was ragged, he saw, and his father stupid and old.

He couldn't shake off this strangeness, which made him dizzy. At night he lay on his back, holding the bed while the stars turned the wrong way. During the day he groped around the village, which was misaligned. He'd left on one side but returned on the other, so now he went wrong among the houses, coming to walls not doors.

Finally the boy understood: he'd walked around the slopes of a great highland and so back home. But the knowledge didn't help. He spilled his food. His drink ran down his chin. He sat by the village yard and held his head, frowning at the villagers until they told him to work.

So he went to the fields, but they sloped the wrong way and made him stagger. His father said, 'Cut down this tree.' The boy swung his axe but it spun him round. He sat down with a bump and gripped the earth. His father helped him up, shouting angry questions, but the boy was useless. His traps caught only his fingers; his arrows clattered among trees and were lost. He hopped in circles, one foot on the spade, leaning too far into the slope or too far out. He pissed on his feet. 'I'll go back around the highland,' he thought, 'and stop this strangeness.'

But then he picked up a hoe, which is a woman's implement. The hoe didn't tip him, so he worked with the wives, trying on their wide straw hats, smiling when they mocked their menfolk. In this way he accepted his strangeness. The village was odd but he didn't care, because his way of looking was as good as another. He crouched to piss, his father baffled and angry.

'Hang on,' said Tom, seeing where this led.

Every morning the father held his son's trousers. The boy put his hands on the old man's shoulders and stepped into the trousers with his eyes closed. If he opened his eyes he fell over. But one day he put on a blanket like a skirt, and left for the fields before his father woke.

'Hang on.'

The blanket taught him how to place his feet – one in front of the other, as on a narrow path, so that the slope didn't fool him. When he came home, his father said, 'You woman!' and punched the side of his head. At once everything was clear.

Tom said, 'Just a minute,' because this was blatantly a story about Johnny, not him.

The boy left home and moved to a house with three women, where he stayed indoors, cleaning and cooking and sweeping the earth floor, which was level and even. He had a delicate way of holding a cup, so that the drink didn't spill.

Later he moved to a town by the river, and then downstream to Canton. Here he met a white sailor. They travelled to London and he left the sailor and danced in Chinese theatres and afterwards bought a boarding house on the Whitechapel Road.

Tom lay with his eyes wide and his eyebrows up. 'So Johnny is back in London.'

18

Mac said, 'I've never been really pally with Johnny. Not like you. But what the hell: it's a come.' A small grin with his small mouth: 'God, Tom, you look rough.'

Mac did complicated things with his ciggie that Tom couldn't bear to watch, various flicks and twirls, and the head thrown back to blow out smoke. Then the same flat brogue, cutting through the clamour in this City pub: 'Of course what we want is both of them. May and Johnny. Three in a bed, me in the middle. Wouldn't know which way to turn. Them in their naked nuddy. Sort of before and after.' His ciggie arm now stiff down, the wrist cocked, black hairs curled over a gold signet ring, and the same numb stare, that didn't change even when he punched you.

Six months since I've seen him. His thickened face, thick thighs in some kind of pin-striped wool, the morning shave already growing out on his thug's neck. 'A good move anyway, shagging a Chinky. Careerwise. But bloody Johnny isn't talking to me. Doesn't answer my calls, anyway, the mad tart.'

Tom managed to say, 'You called the takeaway?'

'Christ, no. Left messages on his mobile. No, his dad'd kill me. Young May not too friendly, either. Maybe she can read minds. Or dicks.'

'Hang on,' said Tom, feeling helpless. 'I should have told you. Johnny is dead.'

'What?'

'Bloody killed himself.'

'Wow.' He stared at Tom, very interested. 'His dad. His dad, you know, found us.'

'What?' said Tom.

'At the takeaway.' Mac nodded, too entertained to smoke. 'He's really dead? Christ.' Filing this away as part of his own legend. 'Well, yes. He called me so I went round. Very odd. I thought the trollop hated me.' Again he showed his bright small teeth. 'Tom. The state of you. What happened?'

'You went round. Then what?'

'Well. I was out with the guys from the office. Friday night. In here, in fact. They'd buggered off and I was feeling sad and lonely. Then Johnny phones. He says blah-blah-blah, so I hop in a cab. Stayed the night. Very nice. Highly recommended. But then you know all about that, I believe.'

Tom looked out the pub window. This was Mac's secret: so casually nasty you were powerless. 'So his dad finds you on the Saturday. Then what? What about Johnny?'

'Dunno. I mean the old man bursts in, fit to kill. I was shitless. You know, mad coolies steaming up from the kitchen. Me in the fridge with the Alsatians. I got dressed sharpish. Johnny looked poleaxed. Sat in bed crying while I'm panicking. I couldn't get any sense out of the silly slot, so off I fucked.'

'Hang on. Crying?'

'Upset about you and May, as you doubtless know. Then little me turns up. Then his monster dad. And I'm thinking I might be next on the menu: number 28, round-eye bollocks. So I creep downstairs and dive over the counter and out the door and back to England.'

'How did his dad know about you?'

'A mystery,' said Mac. 'Though that was a hellish squeaky bed.'

'Did you tell anyone about . . . I don't know. About me.'

'No.' Mac laughed. 'Wait. Is that why you fell out with May? Really?'

Wearily Tom said, 'Anyway, that's when he died. That Saturday.'

'No doubt. Shagged by the master. Nothing else to live for.'

'Christ.'

'Sorry, Tom. A joke. He was a pal, et cetera.'

'What a shit.'

'They do say so. But, you know, we should be friends, you and me. Who else can we trust?' He winked: 'Long-time buddies.'

'Fuck off.'

Mac laughed. 'But you saw Charlie, poor bastard. Him and his lovely fiancée. I mean the bite goes deep. Nothing else will do. What's up? Don't go. Sit down, you pillock. Just have a half. A coffee, then. Come on, you dick, don't be boring. You still at that squat? Don't go, you prat. Tom?'

*

He lay in the doss bag, his cut ankle throbbing, trying not to think about anything except the van: no rope for the back doors, and the tank was low. 'I should pick up my dole. Or get a job.' He shuddered, remembering The Dream House. A different kind of takeaway, then: Indian or a pizza place maybe, anything with a bike.

Then he thought, 'Of course,' because he remembered when the bad thoughts started. They'd started on his last night at the takeaway.

He'd been stoned and scared. He'd bought an eighth in Brixton, rolling joints in pub toilets, but then it was work time so he'd swallowed the rest. He was walking to Brixton Tube, cruising nicely thank you, no one would know, when it was like a bullet went past. He stopped on the pavement thinking, 'What?' He struggled on, then leaned against a wall, laughing till he was bent double and tasting his sick, because the pretty women were saying:

'You want me but it's not my fault.'

'I lift my nose over my body, which is the least of me.'

'I'm in a hurry, because I'm a person of business, not beauty.'

'It's *tiring* to be cute.'

Onto the Tube and he'd leered at Londoners: a big-leg lezzie; pretty, skinny little-tit women who are often mad; an obvious perv, who doubtless chats up children in parks, doubtless with smiles and conjuring tricks and a neatly prinked pink-tinted miniature poodle; sad bachelors that piss / At midnight in their bedsit sinks. But suddenly everyone looked Chinese, which wasn't funny at all.

So then it was The Fear. He'd struggled out of the Whitechapel Tube, his hand on the tiled walls, flinching from other people – their boiled hands, the meaty heads squeezed from their clothes, but above all from the women in jeans. Down the Whitechapel Road and into the takeaway, but here it was lizard evil – Wei and Chung quiet and blinking, Mr Tan checking the scripts, tapping the tinfoil packs, his crocodile calm, and Tom, sick with The Fear, knowing that the food was full of horrors.

With a jeering grin Wei had given him the packs, and he tottered to the bike, queasy at the smells of food. At the first address he knocked softly and no one came. Then an old woman answered with a smile – so she wanted him inside for grisly old-person sex. At the next drop the hall light was red, with a roaring from the living room like sinners on spits, and he nearly legged it while the man went for his money. 'You all right, mate?'

'Yes,' he whispered. 'Why?'

Then a Chinese child, sex uncertain, Tom ashamed because the packs were hot as turds, but the child smiled and shut the door. Tom stumbled off, picturing the youngster inside, dragging its satin slippers over Turkish rugs, sticky with opium, and into a gloomy bedroom where its master stands, shaking with sick dependence, takes the pack two-handed, hurries to the lamp, with coiled mandarin talons rips the lid, and drinks the filthy liquid while the sulking child, watching from the shadows as its master swoons, pockets a costly trinket and is gone, the cat-flap wagging and it's free at last.

'You druggie dickhead,' Tom had said, leaning against

the bike, heart galloping, shaking his head in wonder. He rode down tenement canyons (bodies in bin bags), through cobbled courtyards (where the Ripper crouched), along a dogleg alley (puddles deep as wells), and food was crawling out the box and up his back. 'You prat.' He was taking a favourite shortcut when the alley narrowed like a funnel. It was only bad-dope bollocks but he could still crash.

'Pillock,' he said, and propped the bike against a wall. He couldn't touch the food, which was sick and spit and shit, so he found a sodden magazine and lifted out the packs. He flopped them in a corner and pushed the bike to the takeaway, muttering, 'The food got stolen. I was on a delivery and I got back to the bike and . . .' But the back door was locked, then Wei and Chung edged him onto the Whitechapel Road, the doss bag full of his stuff, and May wouldn't see him, and upstairs Johnny had the scissors.

So now he lay in the van, thinking, 'Of course,' because he'd seen first of all that the dreams showed families like the Tans, with maybe an outsider like himself. Then that there were people losing their bollocks, just like Johnny had stabbed himself. And then how the dreams had started in the mountains, where the river was small, and had travelled downstream and finally to London. And here was the final clue, which showed him when all this bad stuff started: it started while Johnny was dying.

19

He hated daylight so he took the Tube. But they hit the
outskirts and the train came up from the dark, clattering
and small, past football fields and ratty trackside trees,
the light coming in and Tom defenceless.

Willesden. He climbed out of the station and into
suburbia: big prams, a hardware shop that spilled across
the pavement, a London bus looking lost, and Tom
squinting under the milky winter sky, weary and sick as
he turned into a side street, everything spread out and
tiring – big houses with big gardens, an everlasting petrol
station – and toiled uphill on the empty afternoon pavements.

'Enough, Johnny, you bastard.'

Then the temple, a large brick box with mock-Gothic
windows and the words 'Methodist Mission' cut into a
stone slab across the eaves. By the gate, though, a concrete
wedding-cake fountain, set with mirrors and coloured
tiles, squirted into the cold. It splashed his pants as he
crossed the big front yard, half builder's rubble and half
tussocky grass, and rang the bell on a cheap plywood
door. 'Dad is praying for me in that place in Willesden,'
Johnny had said. 'He wants the spirits to put me back on
the straight and narrow-minded.'

'Stupid, his jokes,' thought Tom. Then the door swung back. A Chinese monk, young and happy in his orange robes.

Tom said, 'Hello. Hi. I'm a friend of John Tan.'

'Ah.' The monk was puzzled, though his huge smile didn't change.

'John Tan,' said Tom. 'He died. He's here, I think.'

'Ah! Tan Yiu, I think. English name John.'

Tom was very shocked. He'd forgotten about the different-names thing. His friend taken by China. 'Can I visit the ashes or the urn or whatever it is?'

'Please. Yes.' The young monk trying to be grave, thick lips squeezing his smile.

At first the place was only damp-smelling corridors: low ceilings, whitewashed dented walls, and the monk's happiness flooding back as he trotted in front, shaved head rocking, his legs and arms ebullient, sandals slapping the floor that changed from ragged mats to parquet to worn lino and back again. 'Tan Yiu ahead. Special room for ashes.'

Then a huge surprising hall, quite empty, where North London clerks had knelt, worried that their worn soles would show, starched collars chafing their boils, but now it was Eastern tat, the arched ceiling in brash colours, scattered mismatched mats, and a wall of ranked godlings, fat and gilded, with demons and beasts and all that Buddhist bollocks, the young monk flashing a big yellow gappy grin over his shoulder, so that Tom said, 'Can you do the kung-fu stuff?'

'We are not fighting monks.'

'No. Not necessarily fighting, hitting. Maybe just smashing bricks and stuff.'

'Not that,' said the boy, surprised but not angry, taking another white corridor, the tattered mats and Third World bareness.

'Whoa,' said Tom. They were passing a room like all the rest – parquet-pattern lino, Gothic windows with Protestant plain glass, varnished tongue-and-groove ceiling – but here a badminton net was stretched between two poles. 'Brilliant,' said Tom. 'Fantastic.' He grabbed a racquet and made a couple of passes. 'God, I'd love to see you killer monks at this. Running up the walls. A bit of slo-mo. Ten foot off the ground. Can you do that? Can you show me? The mid-air stuff?'

'Maybe we go to Tan Yiu.'

Another narrow corridor, the whitewash soft with damp, and the monk walked behind, watching for trouble. But Tom was silenced, because here was a little room to the side.

It was walled with cabinets, each a foot square, so he thought of the locker room at school. But the cabinets were glossy with lacquer, red for luck. They had a fancy strip of gilt around the edge, and in the middle was a brass frame for a picture of the dead. Mostly the picture frames were empty, but half a dozen had colour photos like a passport snap. He saw Johnny's picture and looked away.

'This stuff,' he said quickly. 'It's to bring peace, because he kill himself.' A table under Johnny's cabinet with candles and flowers.

'Kill himself. So family give things – flowers, lights – and also come. They talk to ashes.'

'Unhappy ghost.'

'Maybe unhappy,' said the monk.

'Trouble for living people.'

'Maybe give trouble.'

'Maybe lost,' said Tom. 'Maybe gone to the ancestors, travelling through their lives, maybe the bits like his own life.'

The monk looked judicious, his big lips squeezed shut over horse's teeth, but perhaps he didn't understand. 'Maybe Tan Yiu angry,' he said.

Tom looked at the little picture. Johnny's lopsided smile, anxious and jaunty, the head tipped back but hurt eyes. 'Oh Christ. Oh God.'

Tears at last. Why didn't I cry before?

The young monk stood at his elbow, his worried frown wrinkling up onto his shaved skull, and that Chinese no-smell, like a statue or Johnny. 'His spirit soon well. Resting and peace.'

'Well, no offence, but I don't believe that stuff, you see. No. And his family. I mean, that was the whole thing – his dad. So how can they help? Maybe he just gets more upset.'

'Family come every day.'

Tom was absorbing this when he heard a squawking. But instead of the Tans, a gang of old women bustled in, square in their nylon jackets, busy little legs in neat trousers. 'Cantonese,' he thought. Their eager faces, heads pushed forward, chattering in whispers, eaters of every-

143

thing, and Tom watching fondly through his tears. He saw May grown old, and himself beside her, old and proud.

He turned away from Johnny, grieving for everything, the women stilled by his sorrow. The monk said gently, 'I leave you. Don't worry. Listen: chants.' A cassette machine stood behind the flowers, specked with paint, and Tom wondered what music the monks had played as they whitewashed the walls. 'This all day. Help him.'

Alone with the women, tears on his chin, Tom faced a life-size plastic Buddha. It was fixed to the wall, floating cross-legged over a table laid with stubby candles in cups, flowers in a cheap glass vase, and a tray of offerings – peanuts, crisps, Cadbury's chocolate buttons, a bottle of mineral water. Its long fingers cupped a plastic pearl like a cricket ball. Its bland young face stared over Tom's head at the cabinets behind him.

He turned back to Johnny. 'Leave me alone, OK,' he said, the women watching. 'It's not my fault and I can't help you.'

The photo smiled from its screwed-on brass frame. It was covered by a clear plastic bastard cover thing, which he picked at with a fingernail. He stepped back, frustrated.

At the corners of Johnny's cabinet were gilt metal knobs, the size of a fingertip. He twisted one. It unscrewed smoothly. But underneath was the top of a fat cross-headed stud, bare steel and businesslike, hiding the last of Johnny Tan.

'Bugger.' The ladies watched, heads craning, absorbed but unsurprised because of course white people are odd.

He passed the gilt knob to the nearest woman. She bowed over it with interest – her cropped white hair, her hand strong from honourable work – showed it to the others, offered it back.

'No,' he said. 'A present.' She watched him step into the corridor, and was staring at the knob when he came back with a fire extinguisher. He drove it into Johnny's face.

'Oh,' she said. The blow echoed through the wall of cabinets and boomed down the corridor.

'Noisy,' he said to the women, who'd shrunk into a corner.

Johnny's photo slid to the floor. Tom bent to pick it up but changed his mind. Twice more he drove the red metal into the wood, the plastic cover flying in splinters.

'Strong,' he said. He looked at the wall of cabinets. 'Yes. Good stuff.' Johnny's cabinet had half-moon dents, and a flake of thick lacquer had fallen off, showing the pale wood, which was still solid.

He set the extinguisher down, suddenly tired. He dragged himself along the corridor, the women leaning around the door to watch. He came to another little room, this time a library, and stared for a while at shelves of cassette tapes, books in Chinese, and ragged old airport thrillers. He walked on, very weary, stopping again at the badminton net. He stared at what he hadn't seen before: the two poles stood in cement in old cooking-oil drums. 'From some takeaway, I suppose.'

Another corridor, the whitewash soft as chalk, a noticeboard where he read about classes for English-speakers, and then a trestle table with books laid out for sale and he pocketed one. 'Too big for the congregation, this place. Not enough people to keep it nice.'

At last the plywood door again. He was stepping outside when the young monk grabbed his wrist: 'Why? Why?'

Tom shook him off. This wasn't, after all, a kung-fu monk.

It was a premonition, perhaps. Tom was at Willesden Tube when a train came in from the centre. He ducked behind a pillar and then saw May.

She liked loose clothes. A studenty big black jacket, her lean profile, hair swinging free, and a buttoned-up white shirt, though he'd seen her lovely breasts, little as kisses.

'May.' Her frightened eyes. 'Hello, babe. It's good to see you.'

'Tom. Well. Actually I wanted to talk to you. Did you call your dad? Because a woman phoned. A couple of times, in fact. It seemed really urgent.'

But then she was striding again, Tom hurrying behind up the station steps, saying, 'How are you? I thought maybe you needed your favourite biker again.'

'Actually I wondered if you'd left London. Back to your dad's, perhaps. Or that area, anyway.'

'Enough about my dad. Christ.' Trotting behind as he hit that High Street again, wondering how she could be normal when the dreams were so . . .

She turned on him. 'What are you doing, in fact? Are you going to the temple?'

146

'Yes. Well, maybe. Actually I've just been.'

'Well, you can't come with me. It's a family thing, right?'

'Right.' Fighting the odds he said, 'I'm sorry I didn't see the funeral. The customs and stuff.'

A sigh, resettling her shoulder bag, then striding off, Tom lagging on his cut ankle. 'Dad wanted the old things – funny clothes and so on – but I didn't. So you didn't miss much.'

'Where does his soul go, in fact?'

'For God's sake, Tom. What a question. I mean, what's the difference? You don't believe it, any more than me.'

Here's what May believes: buses stop with their door right next to her – not always, but more than you'd think; she knows what track is playing before she turns the radio on, or maybe they've just played it, or it's playing on some other station; she dreams about friends before they call, and if she phones she can tell if they're at home, or just coming home, or maybe they're actually, you know, thinking about their home; she speaks the truth and gets in trouble for it, but it's her nature, she can't help it and actually doesn't want to help it, because the truth is within, not in churches or books, so you just have to follow your real nature whatever anyone thinks. And when she was a toddler in Hong Kong, they would visit her mother in the cemetery on Pok Fu Lam Road, where the buses halt at every stop, even if no one is there, because the dead might be travelling.

They were passing the hardware shop, Tom dodging

an aluminium ladder, a box of washing lines, stacked rubber buckets, dog food in sacks. 'So who's riding the bike now?'

'We haven't got a bike, have we. Anyway, we use the car. It's better.'

'That bike. We went everywhere. That first time, as well. Do you remember?'

'People stole the food.'

'Not from me. Not when I was doing it.'

'No, but it's happened. And someone set fire to a bike once. Before you started, maybe. Maybe you didn't hear.'

'It was sweet for us, though.'

'A car is better. Dad's friends have swapped as well. I mean, he needs the car anyway, so a bike's just an overhead. And he's told the police.'

'What? That it got stolen?'

'For the insurance.'

'Did he mention me, do you think?'

'I think so. Probably. Yes.'

They were outside the temple and she felt safe. She looked him in the eyes and said firmly, 'Goodbye, Tom.'

He thought, 'Let her go: if you let her go she'll come back.' But then he followed her into the yard.

'I said goodbye.'

'Yes. Well, I'll call you.'

'Don't call. I mean it.' She was angry again. 'And what about you trying to break in? What was that about? And look at you: like a tramp.'

He said, 'May, I know what your dad thinks. I mean,

did your dad talk to you about me? I know he doesn't like me at the moment. Because of me and Johnny.'

'And?'

'But I just want to tell you that he's wrong.'

'Really? That's not what I heard.'

Tom put his hand to his forehead. 'All right. But it was a kids' thing. I was upset, that's all.'

'Fine,' she said, quite calm. 'That makes it easier.' She turned and walked away so that he said, 'I keep dreaming about you.'

She stopped and scowled at him down the cracked concrete path. 'I know.'

'Really? You felt it?'

'Wei told me. I don't like it. It's not flattering, if that's what you think. We're not together any more. And never will be.'

'It's nothing bad. Not what you think. Bloody Wei. I mean I felt closer to you, through the dreams. Like I was trying to understand about you and your family and me. But then I wasn't so sure. The dreams were too strange. So now I think maybe my dreams are getting mixed up with Johnny.'

'Right. So actually you were dreaming about *him*.'

'No. Christ. Why do you say that? No, it's just. I don't know. I think maybe Johnny sees something in the after-life, and then I dream about it. Or maybe I'm dreaming already and things he sees in the afterlife get into the dreams. I can't work it out.'

'So. Dreams about my brother. Very, very funny.'

'You have to save me. I need saving.'

'From what, for God's sake?' He didn't answer, and she said, 'Yes, really funny. Wet dreams about a dead person.'

'Don't, May. I love you.'

'Don't say that. Don't you ever say that. Don't come near me, or dream about me, or dream about Johnny. Maybe he doesn't like it either.'

20

Tom paced Willesden station, hobbling fast on his bad ankle, waiting for the cops or a gang of fighting monks to abseil in. He thought of May with the young monk in the room of ashes. They were staring at the dented wood. Tom screwed up his face: 'Johnny gets cremated and I fetch the fire extinguisher.'

On the long Tube ride he sat dumbly, wiggling his toes in the wet canvas shoes, his toenails showing through the holes, not thinking of anything except the van, parked by Waterloo station and probably covered in tickets again.

He could beg. He could buy petrol and drive and drive until the trees met overhead, and leave all this city stuff and the dread in his belly.

'No Chinks in the country.' He pictured fat Mr Tan on tiptoes in a muddy lane, helpless in his trodden-down shoes. Although, come to think of it, Tan was an ex-peasant, knee-deep in buffalo shit. 'Actually, I don't know anything about the bugger.'

Suddenly he understood May. She wasn't something in a dream. She was a real person, angry in a street in London. This was important. She was lovable because she was real. He was humbled by this insight, and glad to be humble.

'We were talking, so we can talk again.' She had jumped on the bike on that first night, eyes like the light on an empty cab, passionate and ready. She'd said yes with her legs in the room under the eaves, the pigeons restless on the slates. When she ate she wiggled her toes, couldn't stop although he laughed. When she turned over in bed her hand was stiff like a swimmer's.

He saw her as a Red Guard. She was holding the little red book of Chairman Mao, looking up, full of joy, red ribbons on her two little sticking-out pigtails. She had a blue padded suit. She held up the book at full stretch, which pulled her trousers up tight. She thought of people looking at her pulled-up trousers.

'I'm going the same way as Gilly.' Or his dad on the bath edge, big Ellie stalled in the door.

He leaned his forehead on the Tube window, so he could watch the black tunnel walls and think about getting out of London. The shaking of the Tube was like the shaking of the van. He pictured himself driving at night, lost in the narrow streets around St Paul's.

'No,' he said, and imagined the river. It was black and glittering, glimpsed between office blocks. He steered towards it and found the Embankment, empty in the small hours, and drove through Chelsea and Hammersmith and on upstream. As the van took corners, he leaned over in the Tube. Next to him, a man in a suit looked angry.

He hit a dirt road, and the van skidded over loose stones and through a night-time village with boats drawn up, then climbed a bald hill and down again to the river, which was dark and wide as a lake. He gave the van off-road tyres. He made it a diesel, throaty and strong. 'It needed driving, that's all, to tighten stuff.'

The stones in the road got bigger, the van roared and gripped, and he passed more boats, a house on stilts, and on the far bank was a black cliff with lights high up, which were the houses that folk call 'sky farms'. The road climbed into forested hills, wet and cool, with mist in the headlights, the knobbly tyres throwing up mud.

He felt free, and laughed. 'This is a long road. It's not a wrong road.' The man in the suit edged away.

The Tube took a clattering bend, and Tom felt the road curve around a wooded hill that fell to the river. It was dawn. He drove under dripping pines, rounded a last bend, and there was the village. May was waiting. She stood by her father's house, brass discs on her blouse, a skirt of many layers, and smiled to see him. The man in the suit saw his answering smile, rapt with love.

He got out of the van and the village was perfect – the huts on bamboo stilts among the pines, children gazing shyly from the windows. There were men in the fields, and a woman waved as she climbed the track from the river, a basket on her arm, fish tails wagging. They went to the headman, May's father, and Tom said, 'I'll be your new son.'

A hut was ready. There was a fire against the mountain chill, and May had laid sweet potatoes on banana leaves. He slept that night on boughs of odorous pine, the hut creaking on its stilts, and in the morning she came to him again and never went home.

Swaying in the Tube, he thought, 'It's like the old dreams: me and May, happy together.'

He helped the villagers, loading their fish in the van and driving up the curving track from the river. When the tank was dry he ran the engine on lamp oil, then fish oil, then on the gas from goat droppings. He put the front axle on blocks and drove a pulley, which dragged a sled up the hill and lifted the bucket in the well.

'And I soon learned the language.'

With the horn he drove rooks from their fields, and with sparks from the battery he lit their fires. At harvest-time he shone the headlights into the threshing house, so the men could work all night. They praised the skill of his hands, and it didn't matter that the headman hated him for spoiling his daughter.

How they were in love! Tom wrote poems on fans, to praise her, and he put gauze bags of tea inside lotus flowers before they closed for the night, in the morning making tea with pure water from the well beside the village, and May smiled at that scent of lotus. At night, when his work was done, they lay on pine boughs in the firelight and stared over the treetops, smoking opium until the village lamps went out, and the dogs had ceased to bark, and a thorn bush was pulled across the pig pen to keep out wolves. May said, 'My husband.' And Tom replied, 'Only a China girl will do.'

He said, 'I have seen the Western races, where the prettiest women are only as pretty as boys. And I have seen the blacks, their men so manly that women are driven mad. But then I saw the yellow folk, in whom the yin is certainly the most strong, and therefore I travelled east.

'First I came to Japan, where there was much variety, with dark or light skin, and large or narrow eyes, and the nose with a higher bridge, which many prefer. But the men have a yang trait, which is shown in their hairy legs and manly build, and this is also seen among the women. And likewise in Korea, although their blood is more pure.

'Then I saw the Thais. The southern Thais are lovely, despite the blood of foreigners. But I went north and even the menfolk showed the yin. And also in Siam, where the tribes by the China border are the most beautiful.

'So I came to China, but was confused. Some here seem Caucasian because of the Turkic strain, and some resemble the Eskimo, and there are Chinese of Malay stock who are small and dark.

'But I recalled the Thais, and came south, where the tribes are soft and yielding, filled with the yin, driven by more virile folk to these wooded hills. And so I found you, the most female of women. And your father is as smooth as a wooden Buddha, and surely your brothers are light and slim.'

'Ah, my family,' said May, her eyes downcast. 'I had a twin, but twins are unlucky so my mother died and then my brother also. And now my father has sent me from the house, because of you. But I am happy to lose him, and would stay with you always.'

'Yes,' said Tom. 'Always.'

In the morning he smiled again, and they kissed as he

left the house. But then he saw the van. It was parked by their hut under a dark pine, whose fallen needles stained its roof. The windows were edged with green, which was moss. He took the jack and worked all day to move a neighbour's broken roof beam, and then with the tyre wrench he levered the new beam home, but the jack and the wrench were rusted. He came again to the van and someone had laid a sickle on the bonnet and scratched the paint. Chickens pecked between the soft tyres, and one stood on the driver's seat, its lime on his coat.

He filled the windscreen washer and thought, 'Why did I do that?' Then May was standing beside him. She said, 'You took me from my father, and now you are restless.'

'No,' he said.

'I lost my home for you,' she said. 'No man will want me, being used.'

'No, no.' But then he thought: 'Perhaps there are women more female, more smooth and slim, in the higher hills.'

Dozing on the Tube seat, Tom half woke. But for once the story wasn't taking over. In fact it all made sense. If you were in China, with all those Chinese women, of course you'd look around, even if you didn't do anything. So he watched himself in the village again.

It was morning, and he was moving the van from their hut. He parked under trees on the far side of the village, thinking, 'In love, only selfishness is wise.' In the afternoon May came to him. He was lying on a bed of pine boughs in the van, warmed by a little charcoal stove that he'd made from river clay, and looked up with surprise.

She laughed and said, 'Won't you speak? Are you shocked? Are you thinking of our time together? You were happy, I think. Would you like that time again?'

Tom shook his head.

'Very well,' said May. 'Very well. But I've a friend who wants to be acquainted, as you and I were acquainted.'

'I'm happy alone.'

'But didn't you want a lover who is slim and smooth and light? This one is all those things, and will do whatever you ask, even favours that were denied elsewhere.' Tom was startled, recalling a small thing he had wished for, that May had refused.

She laughed and gave him a folded note. 'Go to this village, to a lover who is everything you want.' He saw that she was angry and couldn't be trusted: he wouldn't go to her friend's house.

But in the evening he was restless in the van, the stove shining red on the roof, and he recalled his quest for the feminine. Perhaps May knew a woman who was slim and light and smooth beyond all others. And he might show that their love affair was finished, by preferring another.

So he opened her note, then climbed the forested hill and came to a village hidden among pines. Cautious, he walked between stone houses, lamps flickering under the trees, and found the house of May's friend and studied its dark windows and cracked wall. Faintly in the dusk he saw carved words above the door. They were vague and wavering in the gloom, but at last he saw a verse which might be translated thus: 'Husbands! You are slaves, / Nightly digging your own graves.'

He smiled, because the writer contradicted May, who wished to maintain their connection, against the call of freedom. He opened the door.

In his worldwide travels he had known countless lovely courtesans. And he had visited numberless houses of pleasure: all were richly furnished, but this excelled them all. He crossed a hallway carpeted with silk. Silver lamps shone from lacquered tables.

But the hall led only to marble steps, which descended into darkness. He paused, then went down the steps, where woven hangings depicted love, with a deep carpet underfoot, and screens that glittered with precious stones. He came to the lower floor and crept through the dark, thinking, 'I am unarmed.'

'Who's that?' he said, because his wrist was seized.

He was drawn into a room, very dark. A slight figure pressed against him, and his heart leapt. He laid the creature backwards on a bed, his blood roused by the slender limbs, so smooth and light.

How he pleasured himself! Anger made him take what had been forbidden.

'Are you content?' said his bedmate in the dark. 'Are you contented now?' The voice was cold, and he liked this coldness.

'I'm content,' he said, and gave his lover a silver

bracelet, pretty but not expensive, that he'd bought for May, until her sorrow bored him. Now his least desire was met, so he gave the bracelet promptly, showing that theirs was a business matter.

But their fingers touched and he was inflamed, and must satisfy himself again, the limbs so light and smooth, like his dream of China.

Next day he thought of nothing but the house of pleasure, and was careless in his work. In the afternoon he climbed again to the house, but the door was locked. He returned at dusk but was disappointed. At last in the dark he could hurry again over the rich carpets and down the marble steps, though he was weak from the night before.

He was welcomed without words, and the night was yet more tiring, because he was roused so often to desire, and his bedmate always ready. 'What do you wish, husband?' said the voice in the dark.

Now he was caught. Daylight was an interlude between these raptures, or was a time when the poor human frame might rest, though he lay in the van and couldn't sleep, and at night in the pleasure house he was restless with the itch of love.

Once, in that dark room, he said, 'I must relieve myself.'

'Do it in the corner, because my neighbours hate me.'

'Why do they hate you?'

There was no reply except, 'Do it in the corner.' But instead he crept through the house and down the garden and stood among the weeds.

In the Tube, the man in a suit smelled it before he saw it – a dark patch that spread along Tom's pants. 'Dirty dog,' he said, and moved down the carriage.

But Tom thought he was standing in the dark garden. He was looking into the forest, where there were lights which moved in the dark as if carried. Then the lights approached. Alarmed, he returned to the house and closed the door. But outside were men of the village, who called, 'You will die there!' So he used the jar in the corner.

He said, 'How strange, how strange. When lying in the near-dark – when there is only light under a door or through a crack in the shutters – how often we see our lover's face wavering in the gloom, sneering and snarling, or stained with decay, the eyes like the sockets of a skull. And this latter thought oppresses me.'

His bedmate said, 'Yet skulls are pretty.'

One evening he lay in the van, too exhausted to sleep, impatient for the pleasure house. There was a tapping on the van doors, and May said, 'Are you there?' But he didn't speak, fearing her sad demands. Yet later, after his spasms in his lover's arms, sick from weariness, he thought of his happy time with May and said, 'I should seek a reconciliation.'

But his bedmate said, 'Why should you trust a woman?' and sang a jolly tavern song, beating time with a slim wrist, the silver bracelet jingling, and the chorus of the song was: 'My woman's love / Changed its palate every month.'

He returned to the village, where men said, 'You were

gone for three days, and the village is dark.' But he was too tired to work, and lay all day in the van, and dreamt of the pelvic socket where a thighbone fits, or of the socket of a guttered candle, or of a man digging his own grave, weakening as he digs.

He thought, 'I must rest or die.'

But the hours dragged in the cold, until it seemed foolish to bear this discontent, fretting the feeble body. Slowly he climbed the hill, up through the sodden forest, resting against trees, aching for his lover as a bone aches for flesh, till he came to the stone village, where many lamps flickered, and there was a murmuring and a hidden busyness that was new. But he hurried to the pleasure house, where his strength was praised, and he caressed that side, so smooth and cool, and the limbs so light.

When he next saw the village a week had passed, though it seemed he had spent only a night in that dark room. He bent above the engine, making many mistakes, his former friends spitting on the ground, until night fell and he turned again to the hill.

But he was followed by jeering villagers, and boys threw stones. 'Fool,' they shouted as he hurried through the forest, his coat over his head, and they were close behind when he crossed the stone village, where there was a muttering like anger, as though hidden folk were roused. He came to the pleasure house and slammed the door and rushed through the corridors, which now were bare stone, their furnishings gone, and into the dark room where his bedmate lay and didn't rise to greet him. The villagers struck the door, but his lover answered with another jeering song: 'Do you see death coming / With slim arms like a woman, / His lap / Empty with a woman's lack?'

When he next left the house, his van was daubed with chicken blood. The windows were broken, and someone had smashed his charcoal stove and scattered the bed. May watched from her father's door, but he turned away and waited in the damp woods until he could climb again to the pleasure house.

He wasn't seen in the village for two weeks, though in that dark room it seemed that only a long night had passed. The villagers shouted as he crept to the van, which was a burnt shell, sunk on melted tyres. He sat on the bare wires of the driver's seat in a smell of wet ash, until he heard a battering on the van. He leapt out and found the villagers with sticks, and the headman angry and grinning, so he fled to the forest and hungered all day for the room where all he saw was his lover's smile and the bracelet gleaming.

Yet he was so weak that his bedmate must bend to his lips when he said, 'I begin to guess your secret, but you see that I do not care.'

'I'm glad that I please you.'

It was a month before he left the room, where he never hungered and where a month was like a winter's night. The van was gone from the village, and he followed its tracks to a cliff above the river, which swirled around a glint of metal. He sat on a stump in the forest but couldn't rest, the day cold, mist filtering downwards through the trees, and then it rained, so that he came again to the village where a woman shouted, 'The foreigner!'

Her cries brought the villagers. Over their heads he saw May, who called, 'Don't go again to that house.'

But he didn't answer and was swallowed into the mob, which dragged him to the headman's hut. Here men had gathered to speak of crops trampled at night, and a beating on their doors by bony knuckles, and in the morning the tracks of bony feet. And the pig pen was robbed, though its bars were so close that only a child could enter, but no child could have killed the pig. Also: the sucking out of the eyes of sheep, the chewing of babies' toes, and the biting off of the precious parts of the watchdogs of the headman, though his gold was untouched.

The men shouted when they saw the foreigner, and May's father bent his great arms, saying, 'Our troubles come from where you go nightly.'

Then the villagers surged forward and the headman's guards were overwhelmed. The crowd hurried the white man from the village, and a madman gripped his arm, saying, 'We know who steals male essence.' So Tom was carried up through the forest, the mist very thick, and a roaring from the hidden folk of the stone village, and so to the pleasure house.

Here he wiped his eyes, because the house was now a tomb in a graveyard. Weeds grew on its roof and the door was broken and its bones scattered by the mob.

May was by his side. She led him among the graves,

where he stumbled and saw the loneliness of death. She pointed to weeds, where a skeleton lay white and new, still with its burial clothes. 'That was my brother,' she said.

On its wrist, though, was the silver bracelet, and in this way Tom was broken, as every bachelor is broken at last.

He crept into the forest and lay on the wet ground. When May came he turned away, recalling his lover in the pleasure house, and nothing else would do. He ate grass and bark, and drank water from the stump of a tree. Then May found a husband, a trader from the town, so he went to the river. At night he slept under bushes among fish bones and rats, and in the day he sat in the sun in an old rotten fishing boat on a mudbank in the shallows.

Stale water lay in the bottom of the boat. It was fringed with green, kissed by mosquitoes, and often he leaned forward and stared down and saw his outline black against the sky. Then he would think, 'Everything all along was all my fault.'

By midnight Tom was back on the streets. As he left the cop shop, the custody sergeant gave him directions to Waterloo.

'Sorry,' said Tom. 'Sorry for all that.'

'Next time, if we find you we keep you.'

It was raining. He smelled of piss. As he walked he remembered lying on the Tube floor at the terminal, still locked in the dream, groaning and twitching because he was held by his lover in the dark room. Then the cops had hauled him away, and he'd fought them because they were also the crowd hauling him up the hill to the graveyard. And finally he'd sat in the rotten boat and stared into the stagnant water, but actually he was sitting on the bunk in a police cell, until the cops decided that he'd stopped being mad.

Waterloo. He turned into a side road, nervous about the van, but there it was, faithful under a street light. As he climbed into the driver's seat he thought, 'I could go home.' The roads were empty: he'd be there in an hour, the house dark and locked up, but the catch on the pantry window was loose. He could take a bath. Sleep in a bed. In the morning he'd visit Gilly. Maybe look for a job. It'd be better without his dad. He could make friends. You make friends if you've got a job.

He started the van, thinking about the route out of London. But only fourth gear worked. He slipped the clutch, the engine toiling as he pulled away, Tom blushing in the dark because his life was crap.

He was turning into Kennington Lane when the clutch burned out. Shouting, revving the engine, he beat the steering wheel as the van rolled gently to the kerb. He put his arms on the wheel and his head on his arms and said, 'The end.'

He'd been wrong about everything. Wrong and wrong, ever since Wei and Chung had pushed him out of the takeaway. But the young monk had put him straight: 'Maybe Tan Yiu angry.'

Very depressed, he climbed out into the rain and went

round the back. But he got a shock when he opened the doors: his doss bag was crooked in the dark, like someone was lying inside.

He got in and closed the doors and sat with his back against the cold side of the van, eyeing the bag. The street light here was faulty. Its yellow light flickered through the windscreen and past the edge of the curtain and lay in a ribbon across the doss bag, which was all bright ridges and black valleys, with Tom watching angry and afraid.

But he was cold and wet. The bag was empty or full or lumpy with bones, but at last he had to slip inside.

He lay there for days. Mostly he dozed, but sometimes he woke to the slap of parking tickets. Then he'd roll asleep again, deep in his last dreams, which were all about Johnny.

21

Johnny was in a mountain pass. He lay on a stony slope, facing a stony slope, mist streaming between. White birds were crossing below him. One by one they hurried across the pass, hopping from rock to rock on their long legs, hurrying because they were afraid. Sometimes one stood on a boulder to rest, upright like a man. Then it would see him and scurry on, though it was tired, stretching its long neck, rolling its eyes, long wings trailing, till it vanished in the mist. At last Johnny understood: the birds were too heavy for this thin air. He stood up and followed them. His breath steamed, as did the wound in his belly. Soon he was going downhill. He slithered on loose stones, following a stream. Ahead, a bird stood on a rock. It turned its long neck towards him, then cried out and spread its wings. It leaned out over the slope and launched into the mist, and through its wake he saw a green valley. The stream had become a river. Next to the river was a village with a red tent and a girl who said, 'I'm young and lovely, as you see.'

And this was his journey home, through lives and deaths that conjured up his own.

First he was a fisherman on the river. He lived with his sister in a house on stilts, and they were chaste although they shared a bed. But the stilts rotted and the house fell over and they woke on the ceiling, which meant that anything was allowed.

Then he was a little boy in the mountains. He fell in the well and screamed, but his fat father thought it was a ghost and ran away so that he drowned.

Then he was a landlord's son, and killed himself because his father was stupid. A drunk climbed into his room and the father heard him and put money under the door to placate his son's ghost. The drunk stayed for months, singing and climbing in and out through the window until the father was a beggar.

Then he was a hunter in the forest. A tiger took his sister and he followed the blood trail to a castle and broke in and caught the tiger-lord with his coat off, grey as a rabbit, sitting with his legs crossed, his terrible smile in a bucket. The hunter was brave and fast and killed the tiger and took his sister home but she was bored for ever.

He was a farmer's son. He told his father, 'Buy me an axe.' The father bought an axe, but the son said, 'Why should I cut wood? Buy me a spade.' The father bought a spade, but the son said, 'Why should I dig? Buy me an ox and plough.' The father bought an ox and plough, but the son said, 'Why should I plough? Buy me a horse to ride.' So the father bought a good horse. Finally the son said, 'Why should I work?' So the father killed him with the axe, and buried him with the spade, and ploughed over his grave, and rode downriver on the fine horse.

He was a girl, relieving herself in the forest. A leech climbed inside her and popped out every night to sing and tell stories, so she couldn't marry but it didn't matter because the leech made her laugh.

He was a girl again, relieving herself in the forest. A spider jumped on her belly and itched so much that she married young. Every night she put the lamp out before she undressed, but one night the moon shone in and her husband saw the spider and tried to kill it. The spider bit the girl and escaped and the husband was left with the girl who was neither alive nor dead.

'Please, Johnny,' said Tom.

But Johnny was a little boy by a river. This was in Oxfordshire, where every spring the river floods. It swells across the plain so that river captains are confused and sail their ships over gardens and roads. Then the little boy would sit with his sister on their roof. When a ship sailed down their road the captain would shout, 'Which way to the river?' But the children only laughed, or else they lied because they wanted the ship to run aground. If they saw a ship jammed in a field or a garden, they ran to where the men were heaving on ropes or digging earth from under the keel or taking off goods to lighten the ship, because there was a chance to steal.

One year the flood came early and full. The children woke in the dark. They ran to the window, but fishes were kissing it. They went back to bed but the bed was wet. They ran up and down the landing, but the Thames was there / In silk slippers climbing the stair. They climbed to the roof, and all day they watched the town. People had rafts made of firewood, or they floated on doors. Old men who had bought their coffins paddled them with brooms through the streets or left them tethered to lamp posts while they visited the tea house, sitting on the tea-house roof and smoking their pipes and grinning at the children. But the river rose until the old men paddled away and the children were waist-deep on the roof. The boy held his sister's hand until it was dark, but the river grew deeper and stronger and in the morning she'd disappeared.

The boy called and called across the flood. As the waters fell he climbed down through the house. There were minnows in her chamber pot and an eel in her bath, but the girl had gone. He followed a trail of smooth stones, like the stones in a stream. A thread seemed part of her clothes, and led him through reeds near Shilling-ford. The hem of her dress was shining over stones at Shiplake, but melted in his hand. Someone said / She crossed waist-deep at Maidenhead.

He walked downriver, searching under trees that wept across the water, afraid to look but he had to, wading through reeds and muddy shallows, leaning over bridges by the pretty riverside pubs. And a great fish / Spawned in his image under Chiswick Bridge, / Where Thames, a lissom country girl, / Comes to London's corseted curves.

So he entered the city. He looked everywhere for the girl, although the women were lovely. He slept under Blackfriars Bridge, with the river's kisses and sighs. He traced the Thames tributaries, that run now in sewers, and listened through tarmac to the Fleet, the Westbourne, and the Effra, which sing: 'I am a hidden London river. / Where in a ditch I'd skip and bicker / Only the sick fat dead old / Notice a dip in the road.'

He grew ragged, looking for the girl, and thought that London was flooded. He saw masts passing stately behind buildings, and his sister at the far end of streets, crossing waist-deep, reflected in the water, two-faced like the Queen of Spades, her lower mouth / Working in the water with sneers and shouts.

He was old, and knew things were bad. He crossed the Whitechapel Road, along through Limehouse, up East India Dock Road, and came again to the river, where a Thames barge was breasting the waves. Familiar its figurehead / Watching over dividing depths!

So now he was sure. He walked downstream, because she was riding the river by day and lay on the waves at night, a billow her pillow. He walked past Greenwich Reach, leaving London, dipping a finger in the river, salty now, and night falling. He was tired, his eyes failing, the estuary very wide under the stars, the shining levels and the smell of the sea, but at last he saw her / Blaze on the brackish water, / Her face the moon / That broods above those tidal pools.

'Enough,' said Tom, but Johnny said:

I was a girl. I was walking to my wedding. I was crossing a forest, but there was a witch upside down in a tree, her skirt around her chin. She dropped on me and ate me. She took my clothes and walked to the wedding and pleased the groom in strange ways. She fell asleep with her mouth open and I called from her belly but the groom didn't answer.

I was a girl and found a jewel that had fallen from the moon and hid it inside me and therefore couldn't marry. But the jewel was poison and I shrivelled up and the villagers burned me.

I was born pregnant. My twin brother must have done it in the womb, and I had a tiny baby which became a tiny man that jumped from twin to twin like a flea, and lived in our trousers, poking its head out. We loved the little man, but then we were older and exiled him from our trousers and he died of grief.

I was the wise man to a king, but the king was murdered by his son, who took the throne and would have killed his sister but I turned her into a bird. The son said, 'Where is my sister?' I said, 'She forgot her name and her home. She couldn't speak. She hid from people. This morning she jumped from a cliff and rose to heaven.' When it was safe I turned her back to a girl. We killed her brother and took the throne and were married, but she was always a bit birdy.

I was a rat-killer asleep on a dark road. I was woken by a queen under a silk umbrella and we sported together. She asked for my secrets and I said, 'Well, I starve two rats in a box until one eats the other and gets a taste for rat and kills other rats. Or I sew up a rat's bottom and it's mad with pain and kills other rats.' The queen said, 'We'll do the same to you,' because actually she was the Queen of the Rats.

I was rich, and lived with my daughter in a fine house. One night I woke up shivering because my quilt had gone. I searched through the house and found the quilt on my daughter. This happened every night, so my daughter said, 'At least wash the smelly thing.' We washed the quilt and for two nights it stayed on my bed, but on the third night I woke up and went to my daughter's room and her leg was around the quilt. I burned the quilt, but it stank as it burned. My daughter went to another town and I left the house and slept on leaves in the forest with only my snot for salt.

I was a little boy and thought I was brave. One day a man and his little boy came to the river. The father and the little boy were identical, so the village women said, 'Beware, because they are lizard people.' But I remembered I was brave and played with the son along the riverbank. Then the man said, 'Will you play with my daughter?' The daughter was also identical, so I was afraid. But I thought, 'If they are lizards I'll run into the river and be safe.' Then the father said, 'Come to my house and eat.' So I went into their house, which was a cave on the riverbank, and the brother and sister and father were smiling in the firelight. Then the father said, 'This is my wife,' and the wife was also identical. I ran into the river, but the brother and sister and mother dived after me. The father danced and laughed on the riverbank saying, 'In fact we are crocodile people.'

I was a girl working on a hill and the wind followed me home. I went upstairs to my old husband, but the wind rattled the door. I went downstairs to bolt the door, but instead I went outside and the wind took me like a crowd.

I was an old man on my deathbed thinking, 'At least I never got kicked in the bollocks.'

I had so little food that I only needed one chopstick and I asked for a pay rise and the boss said, 'We already pay rice,' so I came to London and my daughter met a white boy and I helped at the wedding: when I said, 'Stand,' the boy stood, and when I said, 'Crap,' the boy clapped and everyone was happy, so happy.

Johnny is making toast or being toasted. He wears a linen suit, flames in the pockets. He opens his jacket and his fancy waistcoat is flames. His hair lifts in the updraught and is licked off by flames. He looks at Tom and flames come from his smile.

Tom says, 'We're both tired,' but Johnny is a boy on a roof with his sister. In the morning the flood has taken her so he searches downstream and finds a body among reeds. He stands pointing and shouting but people run away. Then they creep back and take the body to a chapel, the boy following. But his sister walks in weeping and he sees that actually he's a ghost and the body is his own and fish ate his precious parts.

So he leaves the chapel. He walks on till he's lost in London. He looks for clues in pavement cracks, street-light flickerings, beer spills and car dents, and the twitches, squints, limps, and shoe-scuffs of passers-by, with only his anger for a guide. He's easily distracted, and follows sirens, a tourist bus with music, police horses, a man in a green hat. For days he's lost in the suburbs and comes to the limits of London, a cold wind over the fields and rubbish in bushes. He turns back through Hookers Road and Pimp Hall Park, along Butcher Row, Organ Lane, Bleeding Heart Yard, Cutthroat Alley, World's End Lane, downhill like water till he finds the river. He's so broken that only ghosts can see him. They're milling clueless on the Embankment. They grab his sleeve and say, 'Up empty elevator shafts, / Floating to closed doors, we weep and tap.'

He tries to pull free, but they carry him along, saying, 'We wander walls and floors / In the Tube's cylindrical corridors.'

They are the lost dead of London. He listens while they sing: 'We ride / Escalator undersides, / Are weary baffled cold / On single-decker buses, upstairs alone, / And can't get home.'

He sings with them: 'Snoring town, / We'll rise through your dreams like the drowned!'

Tom is a little boy. He's playing in a park and finds a house and sees a window among the ivy. On tiptoes he peeks inside and sees an old Chinaman reading. The old man looks up, surprised. Tom is frightened of his evil face, and runs down the side of the house and sees a door under the ivy. He hesitates, then reaches up and turns the handle. He goes down a dark passage and comes to a room.

Perhaps it's the old Chinaman's room because there's a book on the table. It's big and heavy, but little Tom pushes it open. It's full of horrible stories about twins and fathers and the chopping-off of bollocks. After an unknown time Tom shuts the book. He squints through rheumy old eyes. There's a little boy at the window.

Tom and Johnny are living through stories, faster and faster:

A woman touches herself so often that her finger becomes a cock, and a man is the same only opposite and one day they shake hands . . .

A farmer is so lonely that he marries his shears, but on their wedding night . . .

Twins are joined at the groin and the surgeon must choose who gets the dick and he shows them pictures of cars, handbags, shoes, power tools, but . . .

A girl plays with her baby brother and thinks that his dick is an extra length of gut and likes to see it stretch up for bits of meat, so when he grows up . . .

A boy wants to fly and a witch says that his precious parts hold him down . . .

A man has a sex change because he loves women, a slave to the shape / Badged on their belly like the ace of spades, / Or the ace of hearts / If they're redheads, pale as playing cards . . .

A wizard wants a woman but she rejects him so he jumps on her until she bursts and becomes a man . . .

A wizard wants a woman but she rejects him so he tears off her husband's parts and rapes him and jumps on him till he's a man again and the man sleeps with his wife but comes with the wizard's seed . . .

A couple tell the gods, 'We've done everything in bed so in the next life we want to swap sex.' They jump from a cliff and in the next life the woman is burst and the man's parts are rotted off . . .

A man walks round a highland and comes back to his village on the wrong side. He spills his food, and can't find his wife's precious part, and lets men find his . . .

A man is so broken that he can see ghosts. He runs through London saying, 'A Chinaman wants to cut off my bollocks because I love his daughter . . .'

A man is so broken that only ghosts can see him. He runs through London saying, 'A Chinaman wants to cut off my bollocks so he can marry me . . .'

A man dreams about a dead man so often that the man comes back and says, 'You woke me . . .'

A man dreams about a girl but her dead brother comes back and says, 'It was me in your dreams and you didn't know because my parts were cut off or burned off or rotted off . . .'

Johnny is in Brixton looking for Tom. The first pub is ankle-deep in water and the gents is in the basement, the steps going down under water. The next is warm and dry but the flood outside is mooning against the windows. The third is flooded but outside is dry so when Johnny opens the door the water carries him out.

He goes to the squat. He opens the front door, water behind it like letters, and follows the water to the basement steps. The basement is full of water but he goes down anyway. No Tom. He walks to the Tube and goes with the water down the steps, the platform sticky with water, the train pushing a bow-wave, then under the river, aquarium windows, to surface at Kennington. He comes out of the Tube and there's the van.

Johnny says:

On my last night alive I heard you and May through the wall, then the cooks taking you to the pool hall. I slept late, and in the morning Mac wanted to do it again. I was crying and the bed was squeaking but he didn't care. Then Dad's fist on the door.

I cried for hours, and in the end there was only May. I knocked on the wall. I went to her door and knocked again. Finally I went in.

She was sitting on the bed, gripping the mattress. She said, 'You did it with Tom, didn't you.'

'Never,' I said.

'Liar. Both of you.' Bright eyes, like she was enjoying it.

I said, 'No. Really,' but she was watching me. When we were young I could lie to her. But not any more, thanks to you.

I said, 'Did you tell Dad? Just now? About Mac?'

'You and my boyfriend.' Almost happy.

The rest of that day: me in my room, May bouncing up and down the stairs, practically *singing*. And Dad kept banging on the door and I'm saying, 'Go away,' though after all what did it matter?

It got dark. I heard you downstairs, then you went off on the bike, and it seemed like I had no one to talk to and nowhere to go. A bit like you, actually, Tom.

And May didn't think, 'Just a schoolboy thing,' or, 'I'll confront Tom.' Instead she told Dad about us. So maybe, Tom, just a suggestion, maybe she was actually *ready* to dump you.

But here's what I'd like to know. I'd like to know how she guessed about you and me. Was it something in bed? Something you did or didn't do? Or – and this is really, really interesting – is there just a kind of air about you?

Do tell. We're all listening.

22

There was a banging under the van. Tom didn't move, but then the back doors popped open. He crawled out of the doss bag. The van was on a low-loader. A man in overalls said, 'Bloody hell,' as Tom climbed down to the road, dragging the bin bag of Johnny's clothes, the man laughing: 'All right?'

Tom leaned in a bus shelter till it was dark, then went to a pub he didn't know. He sipped a half all night, limping to other tables, opening the bin bag with gestures and nods. Towards closing time he got a pint for a pair of shoes and gave up.

'Drink up, please, pal.'

'All right. Fuck off.'

He went round the ashtrays, taking butts, dizzy but not from the beer, the barman shaking his head. He sat on a bench in the cold and rain and dark, thinking, 'I should have stayed in the van.' Cosy in the car-pound, sneaking out at night, nicking stuff from the other cars.

He hunched under his jacket and rolled the butts in a fag paper. He threw the wet jacket behind the bench and pulled Johnny's from the bin bag. He hesitated, then tucked his jeans in his socks and pulled on Johnny's pants. He thought about fighting the cons for his basement room but instead went north, warming himself with walking, the rain a misty drift under the street lights, every house with a horrible story.

He crossed the river at Tower Bridge, cars hissing on the wet road. But then the cars seemed full of water, the drivers nodding and drowned, so he put his head down and marched.

By Commercial Road he was watching the shops. He walked near the gutter because a shop window could burst out under the weight of water. He edged to a shoe shop and put his head to the glass, hands cupped around his eyes, but couldn't tell and hurried on.

He thought, 'Maybe you know you're a ghost if it's raining and you don't get wet.' He touched his clothes: they were wet, but perhaps that didn't count. He touched his face, but now his hands were wet from the clothes.

The Whitechapel Road. He started across, but in the middle he crouched to touch the white line. He heard a car behind. It swept past, no problem. A car came from in front and he spread his arms, staring into the lights. He walked along the white line, thinking, 'Why can't I feel my bollocks wobbling?' But maybe only a woman would ask this.

He crossed to the pavement, his hand and ribs and ankle sore. He wouldn't look at his hands because the street lights were yellow, and he wouldn't watch himself in shop windows because of Johnny's clothes. He thought that Johnny was looking out of his eyes.

He walked on, showing Johnny the world. They came to the alley behind the takeaway. Snapped washing line hung from the pipes. The dog barked.

Tom climbed the drainpipe, banging his balls to make them ache. He opened his knife and got onto Johnny's window ledge and forced the latch, his hand and ankle bleeding as he squeezed inside.

A faggoty smell of talc and scented soap. He pissed in the sink, saying to Johnny, 'Women can't do this.' There was no mattress on the bed. He put the bedside rug on the bare wires and sat down, thinking, 'The mattress was full of his blood.'

He was desperate for a smoke and thought of the Marlboros under the sink. Hungry, too. A bit of toast.

He heard the back door slam, then someone in the kitchen. It must be May. She started upstairs, again sounding like a crowd. 'She's drunk,' he thought, smiling and puzzled.

There was whispering. As her door closed he heard the voice of the Aussie doc.

He stood up. He opened the door, quiet but quick, and crept downstairs. He thought about Johnny and May going up and down these stairs. He put a hand down his pants but couldn't be sure.

Into the kitchen and he found the cigarettes, thank Christ. He lit up in the dark, his hands shaking. Weak with the hit he went to the kitchen window. Raining still, and the jacket upstairs in the room next to the room with the bed that squeaked. He dropped the butt into the sink and twisted the gas tap, thinking, 'Toast.' He turned on more gas and sat in the dark at the kitchen table, his arms laid flat like May's dad.

'A place I can't stay and can't leave.'

There was a stink of gas so he went through and sat on the tall stool behind the counter, thinking about the dreams and who had sent them.

'I'll wait, and in the morning Mr Tan will come down and I'll tell him I'll work for nothing and be the son he lost.'

Then he smelled gas again and knew it was time.

He put a fresh cigarette in his mouth and went back into the kitchen. He said, 'Thanks,' because Johnny was holding the lighter. It clicked twice without lighting. Then it lit, and the flame was everywhere.

NOTES

The notion of food coming alive in the belly is adapted from a passage on p. 150 of Wolfram Eberhard's *Local Cultures of South and East China* (E. J. Brill, Leiden, 1968), where it is noted that certain tribes believed that a potion called ku had this effect, producing a fatal swelling, after which the soul of the victim must serve the poisoner.

The love token found in a grave is perhaps the most common plot twist in Chinese ghost lore.

Would-be squatters should note that the old house at 1 Canterbury Crescent, where I squatted for six months, has been demolished with the rest of the Crescent and replaced by new houses in private hands.

This is the last of three books about China. 'I'm in China more than I'm here,' says Tom. Often, in the past nine years, I've felt the same.